CROMPTON DIVIDED

Robert Sheckley

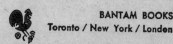
BANTAM BOOKS
Toronto / New York / London

CROMPTON DIVIDED
A Bantam Book

PRINTING HISTORY
Holt, Rinehart & Winston edition published November 1978
Bantam edition / November 1979

ISBN 0-553-12900-7

Published simultaneously in the United States and Canada

*Bantam Books are published by Bantam Books, Inc. Its trade-
mark, consisting of the words "Bantam Books" and the por-
trayal of a bantam, is Registered in U. S. Patent and Trademark
Office and in other countries. Marca Registrada. Bantam
Books, Inc., 666 Fifth Avenue, New York, New York 10019.*

To Abby, with love

ONE

The sign at the side of Route 29 read: WELCOME TO BERGA-MOT, NEW JERSEY, HOME OF PSYCHOSMELL, INC.

The enterprising traveler might have figured that much out for himself by the intermingled fragrances evident even at this distance from the central plant. Even a casual nosologist might well have distinguished cassia and clove, rosemary and cinnamon, sassafras and vetiver, all pierced through by the clear sharp odors of ginger, lemon, and linaloe.

The central plant sprawled on the outskirts of town: a low rambling series of one-story terra-cotta buildings set on some twenty acres of rolling parkland, all surrounded by a double-link constrictor fence.

The guard—a beefy android modeled to look like a heavy-drinking Irishman of the Night Watchman class—looked up when the Sills-Maxwell puttered quietly up, driven by a small man in a plaid oxygen mask. There was a half-second pause while the guard's perceptions took up synaptic slack; and then the android grinned cheerfully and threw a mock salute.

"Well, now, sure and if it ain't Mr. Alistair Crompton, our very own Chief Tester. How's the love life, Al?"

"Go screw yourself," Alistair said. This is a particularly bad insult to lay on an android, since these unfortunates are capable of that anatomical irregularity. But Mike Maginnis did not take it amiss. For five years he had greeted Crompton in the same way, and had received the same answer. Any other response would have confused him.

"That's pretty good, Mr. Crompton, pretty good indeed!" said the laughing pseudo-Irishman, and waved Crompton through.

Five minutes later, after parking the Sills-Maxwell in its customary place, Crompton was walking through the dust-free corridors of Psychosmell, Inc. He had entered at precisely 8:52 A.M., as always. Now he took his customary walk down Lavender Lane, as the central corridor was irreverently named. He nodded to Mr. Demiger, the Chief Macerator, and to Miss Resutte, the Assistant Distiller. He passed the inevitable guided tour, and heard Dominic Spellings, the Company Public Relations Man, telling the little group of tourists how the Yakuts of north-eastern Siberia beat the bark of the storax tree, causing the balsam to exude into the inner bark, which was then removed, boiled . . .

Crompton walked on, past the fragrant storerooms with their bales of cassia, hyacinth, rosemary, peppermint, geranium, and patchouli. He passed the special storerooms for extraterrestrial substances, each storeroom possessing its own controls for air mix, humidity, temperature, and dew point. In these the less costly alien substances were kept: indrigita oil from Cepheus II, chips of cannotia (Nile-smelling before processing in palmerosa oil and ionone), baled leaves of the night-blooming ocepti, and the like.

Beyond this, the corridor branched. Crompton took the left turn and came to the door at the end marked CHIEF TESTER'S ROOM. This was his office, the heart of his little empire within a monopoly. This was where Crompton produced those concoctions that had brought him to the attention of leading olfactophiles, and had made his work a standard of excellence in the field.

His assistant, Miss Anachos, was already seated at one of the testing tables. "Good morning, Mr. Crompton," she said. She was a willowy brunette with hair twisted into the Medusette style so popular that year. Crompton nodded curtly. He had lusted after Miss Anachos every day of the two years she had been working for him. He had never revealed this, of course, because it would have been improper, undignified, and futile: attractive young women were not for the likes of Crompton, who was unattractive physically, mentally, and spiritually.

"Oh, Mr. Crompton," Miss Anachos said. "The big day has finally arrived, hasn't it? *Your* big day, Mr. Crompton. Aren't you *excited?*"

Crompton peeled off his oxygen mask; it was unnecessary in the superclean and hyperventilated air of the plant. He shrugged his narrow shoulders. "It's all a lot of nonsense," he said briskly. "Good for morale, though, I suppose."

"Good for *your* morale, I should hope," Miss Anachos said, speaking in the italics Crompton had grown to loathe. "After all, you're the *star* today!"

"I am not insensible of the honor," Crompton said. "However, congratulations are a little premature. The Board of Directors meets at noon sharp, and it is then that I make my presentation. What Mr. Blount will think of it . . ."

"He will *adore* it!" Miss Anachos said. "You are the best psychosmell contriver in the business, Mr. Crompton, as you very well *know!*"

Miss Anachos's appreciation of his talent—unmixed with a scintilla of regard for him as a man—was beginning to pall on Crompton. He sat down at his workbench and said, "That is as it may be, Miss Anachos. Now to work! Bring me Preparation H. I shall also require the Schedule Four materials."

"Yes *sir!*" She swished past him, and Crompton caught a fleeting impression of the seminatural fragrance of her skin. Christ, he thought, I wish I could bottle *that!* Then, resolutely, he put his mind to the work at hand. A lot was riding on the job he turned out in the next several hours. Just how much, not even Miss Anachos could know.

The power of smell to elicit memory was well known to antiquity. Hermippus of Smyrna relates, in his *Botanical Researches*, how King Pherecydes of the Thessalonians paid two hundred talents of silver for a thumbnail-sized fragment of Arabian anicerys, which, compounded with myrrh, frankincense, and powdered oryx horn, and mixed with Hurcanian mead, kindled in the partaker a vision of a vast and gloomy marble hall set on a high mountain in the Caucasus. In Babylonia, before the Hittites, skilled thaumaturges cured plague and schistosomiasis by skillful concoction of odoriferous substances. In China, an oil pressed from night-blossoming asphodel, treated with silver, powdered ebony, and lotus root, wrapped with red willow leaves and stored for ten years in a granite chalice, was reputed to give a man the ability to remember his face before he was born.

It was not until the twenty-first century, however, that the capacity of odor to elicit memory, dreams, and visions was popularized, systematized, and commercialized. The reason for this was the sudden availability of extraterrestrial odoriferents with unusual and dramatic qualities. Dalton's expedition to Slia II brought back agania root, hkpersia, and the now ubiquitous meningiis leaf. Von Ketter's three voyages to the Raschid Worlds introduced sisia, oil of mnoui, and the incomparable attar of brunchioses. These substances were psychotropic: they combined well with certain Terran bases. For the people of Earth, bound to their planet by the high cost of extraterrestrial travel, these substances were a genuine smell of the unknown, an intoxicating luxury, and a bittersweet journey into the hidden recesses of their own minds.

Shrewd businessmen organized the Extraterrestrial Fragrances Guild, and kept it a close monopoly. The moderately well-off could buy any one of a dozen commercial scents, all with memory-releasing powers. The wealthy could go to a firm like Psychosmell, and, for a price, have an expert like Crompton mix an individualized fragrance for them, tuned to the configuration of the yellowish-brown fibers deriving from the ganglionic cells in their olfactorybulb outcrop. A man like Crompton was capable of pinpointing specific olfactory-memory hookups and their stimulators, and was thus able to produce memories on demand.

But Crompton's finest work, his greatest challenge, and the ultimate testing of his skill, came once every five years when the Board of Directors of Psychosmell assembled from various worlds and met at the mother company in New Jersey. For that occasion, it was customary for the Chief Tester to concoct a specific substance for the world's greatest gourmet of smell—the legendary John Blount.

Crompton had full data on Blount's olfactory responses. Working with infrared photographs of olfactory cell output, with catalytic balance levels, with chemical analyses of the aqueous mucus covering Blount's ganglionic cell fibers, Crompton prepared his masterpiece.

No expense was spared, of course, on this day of days. From the deep vaults Crompton ordered up the costliest of substances—oil of redolence from Tarmac II; ten entire fingers of rhzia bark from Alclepton, valued at sixty thousand dollars an ounce; and even sixty grams of the incomparable essence of lurhistia, derived from the buds of the hypervalidation plant that grows only on five acres of hallowed ground on the dingy planet Alphone IV.

These substances, worth a fortune on the blacksmell market, were handled casually on this auspicious day. And Crompton wrought wonders with them.

The concoction could only be made at the last moment, just before presentation; for so volatile were some of the rare oils, so subtle the esters, so cranky the ketones, that the precious essence would transmogrify itself in a few hours.

Crompton labored, and all of the Psychosmell people waited in anxiety, for they would all share in his triumph or defeat. Old John Blount would predicate the bonus for all workers on his mood of the moment. And his mood of the moment would be determined by his judgment of Crompton's concoction.

After the presentation, the plant would close for two weeks' holiday. Just before closing, bonuses would be announced. So Crompton's degree of success could mean the difference between a week on Luna if all went well, and a day in Asbury Park if it went any other way.

Crompton worked, oblivious to the almost palpable atmosphere of strain. Lavishly he mixed in an entire gram of lurhistia—a ten-thousandth of the entire galactic supply! Miss Anachos caught her breath when she saw this: she so *hoped* that Crompton would not overdo the rarity factor, nor rely on the *shock* of expensive alien substances to make his effect. Old John Blount was too wise a fox to be taken in by *that!*

Icy cold, utterly concentrated, Crompton worked away with his balsams, gums, dessicated rhizomes, twigs, bits of bark, leaves, muck sacs, peelings, roots, pressed flower petals, fruits, seeds, and the like. Watching his icy control, Miss Anachos wanted to scream. She was aware, of course, that Crompton was a very special kind of freak, barely human. She didn't know much about it: people said that some sort of unlucky accident had befallen Crompton at birth, and he had been subjected, in his early years, to the now discredited psychomechanical techniques of Massive Cleavage. That meant that Crompton was *missing something*. But what that something was, Miss Anachos did not know, or care. She tended to consider Crompton a robot, without personal tastes or history. Most people thought of Crompton in that way—as a windup man without feelings, without a soul.

They were wrong about this. Crompton was shortly to show them just how much soul he had.

The long black hand of the clock on the wall crept past the quarter hour, nearing high noon. Miss Anachos gritted her teeth. Why didn't he finish? What was he waiting for? Didn't he realize that her *bonus* was resting on the results of his talented nose and quick, precise bony white hands?

At five minutes to twelve, Crompton looked up from his workbench. He held in his hands a plain testing bottle of rose quartz. He said quietly, "I shall arise now and go to the Board Room. You may join the other workers in the Assembly Hall. I will clean up personally, later, as always."

"Yes sir!" Miss Anachos said, and rustled off, bearing with her that common womanly scent more subtle and precious than the rarest of crystalline confections.

Crompton watched her go. No expression crossed his wizened features. He was glad, however, that he had seen and smelled the last of Miss Anachos. Win, lose, or draw, her exudations would never again disturb his equanimity. Yes, he had sniffed the last of all of them! For soon, very soon, the moment would come when he would—

He stopped himself in midthought. Anticipation could be dangerous. He knew what he had to do. It was only necessary for him to do it—cleanly—as a sword cuts flesh.

Holding the precious substance in its refracting quartz container, Crompton left the Chief Tester's Room and made his way to the Directors' Suite, where the near legendary John Blount was awaiting him.

Thirty-five years previously, a male child had been born to Beth and Lyle Crompton of Amundsenville, Marie Byrd Land, Antarctica. Lyle was a foreman at the Scott Plutonium Mines. Beth was a part-time assembler at the local transistor factory. Both parents had a satisfactory record of mental and physical health. The infant, christened Alistair, showed every sign of excellent postnatal adjustment.

During his first nine years, Alistair appeared normal in every respect, except for a certain moodiness; but children often are moody for no reason at all. Aside from that, Alistair was an inquisitive, aggressive, affectionate, and lighthearted child, and well above the norm in intelligence.

In his tenth year Alistair's moodiness showed a marked increase. Some days the child would sit alone for hours, staring at nothing. At times he didn't respond to his own name. These "spells" were not recognized as symptoms. They were passed off as the reveries of a high-strung, imaginative child, to be outgrown in due time.

During his eleventh year they increased in number and severity. He became subject to temper tantrums, for which the local doctor prescribed tranquilizers. One day, at the age of eleven years, seven months, Alistair struck a little girl for no discernable reason. When she cried, he attempted to strangle her. Finding this beyond his strength, he picked up a schoolbook and tried to smash in her skull. An adult managed to drag the kicking, screaming Alistair away. The girl suffered a brain concussion and was hospitalized for almost a year.

When questioned, Alistair maintained that he hadn't done it. Someone else must have done it. *He* would never hurt anyone, he insisted. Beside, he liked that little girl and was going to marry her when they both grew up.

More questioning only succeeded in driving him into a stupor that lasted for five days.

Even then there was time to save Alistair, if anyone had been able to recognize the early symptoms of virus schizophrenia.

In the temperate zones, virus schizophrenia had been endemic for centuries, and occasionally broke out into epidemics such as the dancing craze of the Middle Ages. Immunology still had not developed a vaccine to deal with the virus. Standard technique at this time, therefore, called for immediate Massive Cleavage while the personalities were still malleable; detection and retention of the dominant personality; and sequestration of the other personalities through a Mikkleton projector into the passive psychoreceptive substance of a Durier body.

The Durier bodies were growth-androids with an estimated forty-five-year viability. But federal law allowed personality Reintegration to be attempted at the age of thirty. The personalities developed in the Durier bodies could, at the discretion of the dominant personality in the original corpus, be taken back into the original personality from which they had issued, with an excellent prognosis for successful fusion. But only if the original operation had been performed in time.

The general practitioner in small, isolated Amundsenville was a good man for frostbite, snow blindness, penguin fever, and other antarctical maladies. But he knew nothing about temperate-zone diseases.

Alistair was put into the town infirmary for two weeks of observation.

During the first week he was moody, shy, and ill at ease, with momentary bursts of his former lightheartedness. In his second week he began to show great affecion toward his nurse, who declared he was a perfect darling. Under the influence of her soothing warmth, Alistair began to act like his former self.

Then, without warning, on the evening of his thirteenth day in the infirmary, Alistair slashed the nurse's face with a broken water tumbler, then made a desperate attempt to cut his own throat. He was hospitalized for his injuries and sank into a catalepsy which the doctor thought was simple shock. Rest and quiet were prescribed; they were the worst possible things, under the circumstances.

After two weeks of stupor characterized by the waxy flexibility of catatonia, the disease reached its climax. Alistair's parents sent the child to the Al Smith Memorial Clinic in New York. There the case was immediately and accurately diagnosed as virus schizophrenia in a terminal stage.

Alistair, now twelve, had few reality-contacts with the world; not enough to provide a working basis for the specialists. He was in an almost continual state of catatonia, his schizoid personalities irreconcilably hardening, his life continuing in a strange, unreachable twilight, among the nightmares that were his only companions. Massive Cleavage had little chance of success in so advanced a case. But without the operation, Alistair was doomed to spend the rest of his life in an institution, never really conscious, never free from the surrealistic dungeons of his mind.

His parents chose the lesser evil, and signed the papers allowing the doctors to make a belated and desperate attempt at Cleavage.

Under deep synthohypnosis, three separate personalities were evoked. The doctors talked to them and made their choice. Two personalities were given names and projected into Durier bodies. The third personality—Alistair—was considered the most adequate by a narrow margin, and retained the original corpus. All three personalities survived the trauma, and the operation was judged a limited success.

The neurohypnotic surgeon in charge, Dr. Vlacjeck, noted in his report that the three personalities, all inadequate, could not hope for a successful Reintegration at the legal age of thirty. The operation had come too late, and the personalities had lost their vital intermingling of traits and sympathies, their essential commonality. In his report he urged them to waive Reintegration and live out their lives as well as they could, each within the stifling confines of his own narrow personality.

In an attempt to render any attempt at Reintegration

unlikely if not impossible, the two Duriers were sent to foster parents on the planets Aaia and Ygga. The doctors wished the best for them, but expected very little.

Alistair Crompton, the dominant personality in the original body, recovered from the operation; but a vital two-thirds of him was missing, gone with the schizoid personalities. Certain human attributes, emotions, capabilities, had been torn from him, never to be replaced or substituted. Crompton grew up an unprepossessing youth of meager height, painfully thin, sharp-nosed and tight-lipped. His hairline was receding, his eyes were glassy, and his face remained sparse of stubble.

His high intelligence and talented olfactory sense brought him a good job and rapid promotion with Psychosmell, Inc., and he had risen quickly to the position of Chief Tester, the top of his profession, a job that brought him respect and a very adequate income. But Crompton was not satisfied.

On all sides of him, the envious Crompton saw people with all their marvelous complexities and contradictions, constantly bursting out of the stereotypes that society tried to force on them. He observed prostitutes who were not good-hearted, army sergeants who detested brutality, wealthy men who never gave a cent to charity, Irishmen who hated talking, Italians who could not carry a tune, Frenchmen with no sense of logic. Most of the human race seemed to live lives of a wonderful and unpredictable richness, erupting into sudden passions and strange calms, saying one thing and doing another, repudiating their backgrounds, overcoming their limitations, confounding psychologists and driving psychoanalysts to drink.

But this splendor was impossible for Crompton, whom the doctors had stripped of complexity for sanity's sake.

Crompton, with a robot's damnable regularity, arrived at Psychosmell promptly at 8:52 every morning of his life. At five o'clock he put away his oils and essences and returned to his furnished room. There he ate a frugal meal of unappetizing health food, played three games of solitaire, filled in one crossword puzzle, and retired to his narrow and lonely bed. Each Saturday night Crompton saw a movie, jostled by merry and unpredictable teen-agers. Sundays and holidays were devoted to the study of Aristotle's *Nicomachean Ethics,* for Crompton believed in self-improvement. And, once a month, Crompton would slink to a newsstand and purchase a magazine of salacious content. In the privacy of his room he would devour its contents; and then, in an ecstasy of self-loathing, rip the detestable thing to shreds.

Crompton was aware, of course, that he had been turned into a stereotype for his own good. He tried to adjust to the situation. For a while he cultivated the company of other slab-sided centimeter-thin personalities. But the others he met were complacent, self-sufficient, and smug in their rigidity. They had been that way since birth. They experienced no lack. They had no dreams of fulfillment, no wish for self-transcendence. Crompton soon found that those who were like him were insufferable; and he was insufferable to anyone else.

He tried hard to break through the stifling limitations of his personality. He attended self-help lectures and read inspirational books. He applied to the New York Greater Romance Service, and they arranged a date for him. Crompton went to meet his sweet unknown in front of Loew's Jupiter Theater, with a white carnation reeking in his lapel. But within a block of the theater he was seized by a trembling fit and forced to retreat to his room.

Crompton had only his basic individual characteristics: intelligence, tenacity, stubbornness, and will. The inevitable exaggeration of these qualities had turned him into a stereotype of an extreme cerebrotonic, a driven monolithic personality aware of its own lacks and passionately desiring fulfillment and fusion. But try as he would, Crompton could not help but act within the narrow confines of his character. His rage at himself and at the well-meaning doctors grew, and his need for self-transcendence increased accordingly.

There was only one way for him to acquire the amazing variety of possibilities, the contradictions, the passions, the *humanness*, of other people. And that was through Reintegration.

Accordingly, when he reached the legal Reintegration age of thirty, Crompton went to see Dr. Vlacjeck, the neurohypnotic surgeon who had performed the original operation. Crompton was excited, eager to get the names and addresses of his missing personality components, eager to

Reintegrate, passionately desirous of becoming a whole human being.

Dr. Vlacjeck reviewed his case, checked him out with his cognoscope, fed the resulting values into his computer terminal, and shook his head sadly over the result.

"Alistair," he said, "it is my unhappy duty to advise you to waive Reintegration and try to accept your life as it is."

"What are you talking about?" Crompton demanded.

"According to the computer readout you simply don't have the stability or strength to hold those detached personalities in balance, to fuse them into yourself."

"Other Cleavees have succeeded," Crompton said. "Why not me?"

"Because the original operation came too late. Your personality segments had already hardened."

"I'll have to take my chances," Crompton said. "Kindly give me the names and addresses of my Duriers."

"I beg you to reconsider," Vlacjeck said. "Any attempt at Reintegration will mean insanity for you, or death."

"Give me the addresses," Crompton demanded coldly. "It is my right under the law. I feel that I am capable of holding them in line. When they have become thoroughly subordinated to my will, fusion will follow. Then we will be a single functioning unit, and I will be an entire human being."

"You don't know what those other Cromptons are like," the doctor said. "You consider *yourself* inadequate? Alistair, you were the pick of the litter!"

"I don't care what they are like," Crompton said. "They are a part of me. The names and addresses, please."

Shaking his head sadly, the doctor wrote on a piece of paper and handed it to Crompton.

"Alistair, this venture has practically no chance of success. I beg you to consider—"

"Thank you, Dr. Vlacjeck," Crompton said, bowed slightly, and left.

As soon as he was outside the office, Crompton's self-control began to crumble. He had not dared show Dr. Vlacjeck his uncertainties: the well-meaning old man would surely have talked him out of the attempted Reintegration. But now, with the names in his pocket and the responsibility entirely his own, anxiety swept over him. He was overcome by an intense trembling fit. He managed to control it long enough to take a taxi back to his furnished room, where he could throw himself on the bed.

He lay for an hour, his body racked by anxiety spasms. Then the fit passed. Soon he was able to control his hands well enough to look at the paper the doctor had given him.

The first name on it was Edgar Loomis, living on the planet Aaia. The other was Dan Stack, resident of Ygga.

What were these embodied portions of his personality like? What humors, what stereotyped shapes had these truncated segments of himself taken?

The paper didn't say. He laid out a hand of solitaire and considered the risks. His early, unintegrated schizoid mind had shown a definite tendency toward homicidal mania. Would that tendency be obliterated in fusion, assuming that the fusion was possible? Or might he be loosing a potential killer upon the world? And aside from that, was he wise in taking a step that carried a powerful threat of insanity and death to himself?

His chance of successful Reintegration was small, according to the doctor; but he was determined to attempt it. Even death or insanity could not be worse, or much different, from the way he lived now.

His mind was made up. But there was a practical difficulty. To Reintegrate, he would have to travel to Aaia, and then to Ygga. Interstellar travel was expensive; and Aaia and Ygga were situated half a galaxy apart.

There was simply no way he could get together the considerable fortune he would need for his fares to these distant worlds and his expenses once he reached them.

No *legal* way existed, to be precise about it.

Crompton was an honest and punctilious man. But this was a matter of life and death. In his circumstance, to abstain from grand larceny was to invite psychic suicide.

Crompton was not suicidal. Coldly he came to his decision, assessed the possibilities, and made his plans.

3

With silent tread. Alistair Crompton proceeded down Primrose Path, as the violet-tinted corridor to Executive Country was called. The rose quartz chalice was gripped firmly in his white hands, and his face was unreadable.

At the end of the corridor was a great oaken door upon which was carved a unicorn sniffing a bouquet of spring wildflowers held out by a simpering damsel in a dirndl. This was the coat of arms of Psychosmell, Inc. Beneath it was the proud company motto, adapted from Martial with a trifling change of one word: *Bene olet, qui bene semper olet.*

Soundlessly the great doors swung open as Crompton approached. Crompton entered the room. In front of him, arranged in a semicircle, were six armchairs in which were seated the six members of the Board. In the center of the semicircle, in an armchair one-third bigger than the others, and raised upon a dais, was the legendary John Blount. Founder of the Firm and Chairman of the Board of Directors.

"It's Crompton, is it?" Blount said in his cracked and quavering voice. "Come forward, Crompton, let's take a look at you."

John Blount was old, considering him as a single personality. But from the viewpoint of the average age of his various parts, Blount was not even middle-aged. Over the years, most of Blount's vital organs had been repaired or replaced. Even his skin (shining with obscene pinkness) was no more than ten years old. His brain was original

16

issue, however, as were his ancient and unfathomable eyes that gleamed incongruously in his firm-fleshed young man's face like the eyes of a gila monster poking through a vat of orange jello.

"Well, Crompton, and how have you been?" Blount said, the old man's quavering voice issuing strangely from the strong young body. (Blount refused to have his voice changed; his hands, too, were original issue. Blount perversely maintained that he enjoyed being old and had no desire to achieve a spurious youthfulness. He wanted to be old, but alive, and did what was necessary to maintain that state.)

"I've been fine, sir," Crompton said.

"Glad to hear it, Crompton, glad to hear it. I have followed your career with interest. You have done fine work for this company, my boy, hee hee hee! And now you have favored me with another sample of your talents?"

"I hope it will please you, sir," Crompton said, resisting the sudden irrational urge to throw himself at Blount's feet and grovel abjectly; for this was how the man's presence affected everyone, including Blount's wife, who had calluses half an inch thick on her knees from following her impulses.

"Well, then, let's get on with it, hee, hee, hee," Blount said, and extended a hand as dry and hard-fleshed as the talons of a Nigerian vulture.

Crompton put the quartz bottle in Blount's hands and stepped back.

The Founder unstoppered it and delicately sniffed (with his original-issue nose—for it was a matter of pride and discretion with him not to tamper with the organ that had made him rich beyond the dreams of avarice).

"Now what have we here?" he mused aloud, his nostrils flexing strongly to allow the fragrance to distribute itself evenly across his old, leathery, but still sensitive olfactory center.

Blount was silent for a time, head thrown back, nostrils working like tiny twin bellows. Crompton knew that the Founder was analyzing the concoction in terms of its primary olfactory qualities, separating and judging the mixture of flowery, fruity, putrid, spicy, burned, and resinous odors. After that, Blount could be counted upon to estimate the intensity of the various components, measuring them in olfacties, the unit of smell-intensity. Only after his analysis was complete would Blount relax and permit himself to experience the effect of the substance.

"First impressions—seaside at Point Pleasant, a rosewood bower, desert winds, a child's haunted face, the smell of north wind . . . Pretty indeed, Crompton! And now the initial rebound effect—intensification—sun on salt water—windrows of kelp—silver cliffs, an iron mountain—and the girl, the girl!"

The Directors stirred uneasily to hear that vibrant cry torn from the throat of the differentially juvenescent Founder. Had Crompton slipped up, perhaps not calculated rotating radical?

"The girl," the Founder cried, "the girl in her white lace mantilla! Oh, Nieves, how could I have forgotten you! I see before me now the black waters of Lake Titicaca lapping at the ironwood pilings. That great bird of ill omen, the condor, soars low overhead, and the sun comes but from behind massed clouds of purple and pink. You hold my hand. Nieves, you are laughing, you do not know . . ."

The Founder fell silent. For an interminable minute he did not speak. Then he lowered his head. He was back in the present. The vision had faded.

"Crompton," he said presently, "you have concocted a superb psychic elicitor. I do not know what it will bring to my colleagues. But it has given me a minute of all-too-rare delight. The memory was false, of course; but its very intensity argues that it must have been true for someone, somewhere. Gentlemen, I declare a double bonus! Crompton, I hereby increase your salary, whatever it is, by one-third."

Crompton thanked him. As the quartz decanter was passed from hand to hand he silently left the room, and the greak oak door closed silently behind him.

The news spread like wildfire throughout the offices of Psychosmell. Rejoicing was general. Crompton walked soberly back to his Chief Tester's Room. He locked the door behind him, and proceeded to straighten up as he did after every working day. Briskly he sealed the precious substances and put them in the chute that carried them to the vacuum vaults where they were automatically returned to their hermetic sanctuary.

There was only one change in his routine. He took the

container of purified essence of lurhistia, costliest substance in the galaxy weight for weight. Tight-lipped, unhesitatingly, he transferred its contents to a plain hermetic flask. He slipped this into his pocket. Then he filled the lurhistia container with common oil of ylang-ylang and returned it to the vault.

On his person now were fifty-nine grams of lurhistia— the entire produce of two years painstaking hand-extraction from the scrawny hypervalidation plants on Alphone IV. Crompton had the equivalent of a medium-sized fortune in his jacket pocket. It was enough to pay his fares to Aaia and Ygga.

He had crossed his Rubicon, taken the first and irrevocable step toward Reintegration. He was on his way! If only he could get away with it.

4

"They don't know the patterns they're weaving," the drunk in the red porkpie hat remarked to Alistair Crompton.

. "Nor do you," Crompton snapped. He was sitting at the serpentine bar of the Damballa Club in disreputable Greenwich Village. The jukebox was playing a golden oldie, "Rub It in Your Belly, Baby," sung by Ghengis Khan and the Hunnies. Crompton was sipping near-beer and waiting for his contact, Mr. Elihu Rutinsky, Chief Agent for the F(I)G.

"Of course I don't know," replied the cheerful, flatulent, red-hatted man on the slender obelisk-shaped barstool with the half-empty (or half-filled) glass of Old Pigslopp brand dry-charcolated whiskey clasped in one grimy-nailed paw. "But at least I know that I don't know, which is more than you can say for other people. And even before I knew, I knew that I didn't know that I didn't know the patterns I was weaving. Take our situation, for example. You probably think that I am quite incidental, a mere accessory to your action, an inert visual object for you to rest your eyes upon—eh?"

Crompton didn't reply. He was still gripped in the icy self-control that had carried him from his testing room to the Sills-Maxwell, and so to Manhattan to meet a man who was already ten minutes late. The bottle of lurhistia burned against his side like a harbinger of decomposed belongings. The jerk in the red porkpie hat leaned close to him, breathing the odor of curdled kvass into his delicate olfactory passages.

"*Mi coche no va,*" the man said unexpectedly.

It was the secret password, decided upon long ago in the peaceful days when Crompton had concocted this scheme!

"You are Elihu Rutinsky!" Crompton said in a half-whisper.

"None other, and at your service," the drunk said, casting aside his hat, stripping off his dexmeer-compound face and his drunkenness, and revealing the silvery mane framing the long, mournful face of the elusive and hypercautious Rutinsky.

"One must make sure," Rutinsky said, with a bleak smile. As Chief Agent for Freesmellers (Illegal) Guild, or F(I)G, this man was responsible for the democratizing and deinstitutionalizing of psychosmelling in Albania, Lithuania, and Transylvania. His Guild, though illegal in the United States, was duly registered and paid taxes, as was required of all illegal organizations.

"Quick, man, there's no time to lose!" Rutinsky snapped.

"Well, *I* wasn't wasting any time," Crompton said. "I was here on time. It was you who insisted upon turning a straightforward criminal business deal into a cloak and dagger operation."

"So I've got a flair for the dramatic," Rutinsky said.

"Is that a crime? It just happens that I'm also cautious. Would you condemn a man for that?"

"I'm not condemning you for anything," Crompton said. "I am merely pointing out that you needn't tell *me* to hurry since *I* am not wasting any time. Shall we get down to business?"

"No." Rutinsky said. "You have hurt my feelings, impugned my honor, and cast an aspersion on my courage. I think I shall have another drink."

"All right," Crompton said, "I'm sorry if what I said upset you. Can we get down to business now?"

"No, I don't think you're being sincere," Rutinsky said sulkily, biting at the ends of his fingernails and snuffling.

"How in God's name did *you* ever get to be Chief Agent for Freesmellers?" Crompton asked.

Rutinsky looked up with a sudden dazzling smile. "I got there because I am clever and intelligent and brave and possess a mercurial temperament. See? I have snapped out of it already. Let me see the bottle."

Crompton handed over the bottle, envious of Rutinsky's mercuriality. He promised himself that someday, after Reintegration, he too would perform outlandish non sequiturs.

Swiftly, deftly, Rutinsky took a miniature olfactotalizer out of his pocket and clamped it to the bottle. First he took a qualitative reading to ensure that this was indeed lurhistia. Then, satisfied, he took a reading on quantity as measured by intensity, to make sure that Crompton hadn't added a gill or so of water.

The pointer on the olfactotalizer dial swung around and bent itself in half around the limit pin!

"Yep, it's the real thing," Rutinsky said reverently. He turned to Crompton and his eyes were moist. "My friend, I wonder if you realize how much you have done. With the contents of this one slender bottle, I can release Freesmellers from their corporate embarrassment. In the name of Edwin Pudger, saintly white-haired head of our organization, I thank you for this favor, Mr. Crompton."

"It's not a favor, it's a criminal business transaction. I mean, pay me."

"Of course," said Rutinsky. He took a bulging wallet from his pocket and began counting out notes. "Let's see;

our agreed-upon price was 800,000 SVUs, to be paid in equal parts of Aaian and Yggan currency. At today's rate of exchange that comes to 18,276 Aaian pronics and 420,087 Yggan drunmushies. Here, I think you will find the count correct."

Alistair stuffed the currency into a pocket. Then he stiffened; he had just heard a high-pitched whistling sound coming from the vicinity of Rutinsky's abdomen.

"What is it?" Crompton demanded.

"Transmission signal," Rutinsky said, taking from his waistcoat a subminiature radio the size and shape of a Dodecanese snuffbox. "It's the CEWS special broadcast. One can't afford to be without it."

"What in God's name is the CEWS?" Crompton demanded.

"Criminal Early Warning System," Rutinsky said. "Didn't you know about it? Let's listen to what they have to say."

"Good afternoon, fellow criminals," a cheerful voice declared over the subminiature quadrophonic speaker. "This is your old friend and d.j. Jack the Ripper broadcasting to you on various clandestine frequencies from our secret mobile unit somewhere deep in the Sangre de Cristo Mountains of romantic New Mexico. Got a good show for you felons out there; latest bank robbery scores on the hour, and, of course, our Opportunity Line which presents daily a list of Golden Sucker Cities where law enforcement has gone lax, or venial, or just plain nonexistent! Tonight's show is brought to you by Footpad Tailors, inventors of the Overcoat with a Thousand Pockets; and by Martin and Mishkin tempered steel burglar tools, and Old Heidelberg cyanide tablets for the job that goes sour. We'll be hearing more about these and other fine products later in the show. But right now I've got a hot flash: An impeccable source from within the organization tells us that Pyschosmell, Inc., the monopolistic octopus of the fragrance world, has been knocked over to the tune of fifty-nine grams of lurhistia, most precious substance weight for weight in the galaxy! The name of the suspect has already been announced, so we break no confidences when we say: Alistair Crompton! If you can hear this, you haven't gotten far enough away! Good luck, Alistair, you're going to need it! And now a selection of tunes from *The Beggar's Opera*. . . ."

Rutinsky turned off the radio. He said to Crompton, "Bit of sloppy planning, eh?"

"It's impossible!" Crompton said. "The business was to shut down for two weeks! Nobody ever checks up on me! I don't understand—"

"Understanding is a luxury you can't afford right now," Rutinsky said. "Good-bye, Crompton. If you're caught, tell them that Rutinsky sneers at them."

So saying, the Chief Agent drew a zero-null hyper-energizing quickcloak out of his pocket. Quickly he shook out the folds of the stolen garment (for it could be carried legally only by FBI men of Ultradon category) and arranged it around his shoulders. Instantly he vanished. Only his red fox porkpie hat was left on the bar. The Mark of Rutinsky!

Crompton paid for the drinks and flung himself out into a hostile and unpromising world.

5

"Alone with you at last, my curvaceous darling—and now, the foam!"

"Would you mind turning off the radio?" Crompton asked.

"Not a chance, buddy," the sweating pedicab driver snarled. "I always listen to the 'House of Chagrin,' my favorite show."

"Let me show you how they do it in Djibouti," the radio warbled, *"with butterflies!"*

Crompton leaned back, trying to keep his composure.

What had happened? How had they gotten on to him? Did
he have a chance now? His destination was the New York
Spaceport situated in what had been Brooklyn before the
interdiction. Already he had gotten as far as Stone Street
and Avenue J, with no pursuit in sight. Only a little farther
now. . . .

*"Ditmas, for the love of litmus paper, get your hands
off my giggie!"*

Now the taxi was rounding the William Bendix Memorial. The doubleshotted circumvex towers of the Spaceport
were just ahead! But now traffic was clogging the road—
bicycles, pedicabs, tricycles, men on roller skates, women
on pogo sticks, persons jogging—all of the variegated trans-
portational forms that made New York famous as "The
City of the Sweaty Thighs." And now, just ahead, the main
gate!

"Rutabaga? Surely there is some simpler explanation."

"Driver, let me out here," Crompton said.

"That'll be five and six."

"Graustark? I should think not!"

"Haven't you got anything smaller?"

"Keep the change!"

*"Denigration is for beginners, my poor Sylvie; the ex-
perienced man likes his mot juste so."*

Leaping from the pedicab, and narrowly escaping
being run over by a walrus-bearded man driving an oxcart,
Crompton rushed through the main gate, trying to look like
a man who was about to miss his spaceship, which, indeed,
was his situation. He rushed past the Disneystand and the
hard-apple salesman, swept by the Punishment Boutique,
and came huffing up to the Trans Pan Interstellar Space-
ways System (TPISS) desk with its proud slogan, *Non est
ad astra mollis a terria via.*

He presented his deckle-edged reservation voucher to
the android made up to look like Albert Dekker. "Ah, so,
velly good," the android with the mismatched voxtape said.
"But you gotta pay, Jack! No payee, no tickee, and no
tickee, no splacefright."

"Of course I'm going to pay," Crompton said. "Would
you like it in Aaian pronics or Yggan drunmushies?"

"We only able to glet Getelguesan fioavics. Uranian
contemptuous, or American Express traveler's checks. You
no glot? Blank change you money, okay, Joe?"

Crompton rushed to the bank, where a nubile exchanger from Drumghera IV deftly made change with her opposed and replicating lips. He sped back to the TPISS desk and presented his money to the android.

"Very good, sir," the android said. "Sorry about that pseudo-Chinese voice earlier. My consistency-autochecking circuits have been malfiring recently and I just haven't gotten around to seeing the electronician. Those fellows cost a fortune and always send you on to a specialist anyhow. So I put up with it, what else can I do on my salary? And usually it's okay, but today as my lousy luck would have it the sunspot cycle coincided with an old Fu Manchu movie in the upper lounge, and photosynthetic diffraction did the rest, and so I came on like an absolute fool—"

"My tickeee!" Crompton gasped.

"Here it is sir," the android said. "First stop is Aaia. You've got ten-year stopover privileges. The standard lunches are served, and you may purchase psychedelics when the craft is in space. Did you ever see any of Albert Dekker's movies? There is an Albert Dekker festival playing now in the south lounge which you are cordially invited to attend—"

But the android moonlighter (he had rented his features to the entrepreneur of the Albert Dekker festival—a move that could have cost him his job if the "own-face" rule had been strictly enforced) no longer had anyone before him, for Crompton had rushed off.

"Crompton, *Crompton*," the android said, and a faint moue of concentration creased his brow. "Ah, yes! Rhymes with Pompton!" And he turned away, satisfied. Androids are never unhappy for long.

Humans, and especially those whose humanotypes can be subsumed under the aegis *Crompton*, are frequently unhappy, and frightened as well. Pale, out of breath, his thighs sweating (like all New Yorkers). Crompton rushed to the entrance gate. As he approached it, someone caught his arm in a vicelike grip and pulled him to an abrupt halt. Crompton looked up into the flattish yellow face of an enormous android gotten up to look like a homicidal maniac.

A thin, shivery voice nearby said, "All right, Toto, hold him but do not break him, yet. I want to talk to this fellow hee hee hee."

Crompton's heart fell into that infinite pit of emptiness that was his stomach. Despairingly he turned and looked into the ancient eyes and at the modern skin of John Blount.

6

"Well, Alistair, and what do you have to say for yourself?" Blount asked.

Crompton shrugged. Not twenty yards away was the entrance gate to his spaceship, tantalizingly near, impossibly far away.

"Nothing much," he said. "How did you find me?"

Blount smiled pityingly. "Only the top executives of the company know the full extent of our security system, Alistair. Special sensors are located in the vaults to register the quantities of the more precious substances present. The quantitative data is fed to a computer, which compares it with continuously upgraded data giving the proper, or formal quantity that should be present at all times. Discrepancies of more than a gram are flashed immediately to mobile security, and simultaneously to me. When I looked over the situation I saw that you were the only possible culprit, and I decided to handle the situation myself."

"That's interesting, I'm sure," Crompton said. "But what happens now?"

Old John Blount smiled his ghastly death's-head grin. "Now, Alistair, I think it is time for you to throw yourself upon my mercy."

Alistair was beginning to tremble. Then he noticed

that he was beginning to tremble. A frown crossed his face, a frown of puzzlement. He was acting afraid of this man who held his life in his hands; but he really didn't feel afraid of him. For after all, Crompton knew that he had taken his chance as a man must do. That he had failed made no difference, finally. What mattered was that he had done his best.

"I doubt very much whether you have any mercy," he said levelly. "So I'm not going to throw myself on *that*. I think I'll just tell you to go screw yourself, and leave it at that. Go screw yourself, Mr. Blount."

Blount's face registered psychopathic amazement, idiot incredulity, moronic disbelief. He stretched out one hand blindly toward Crompton. Strangling on sputum and rage, he cried, "You—you—"

"Hee hee hee," Crompton said scornfully.

Toto reacted to his master's distress by swinging up his great fist, preparatory to splattering Crompton all over the wall. Crompton winced, but his eyes did not blink and his mouth did not twitch. Blount called out, "No, don't hurt him!"

Toto pulled the punch just in time, and suffered a double hernia from the sudden g-strain.

"Crompton," the old man said, in a voice as light and faint as corn silk blowing over blue plastic, "do you know what the penalty is for your crime?"

"Haven't the foggiest," Crompton said.

"Ten years in prison."

"I can do that standing on my head," Crompton retorted.

"No doubt you can," Blount said. "That is why I am not going to have you arrested."

"You're not?"

The old man shook his head and smiled a tricky smile. "You are free to go, to the ends of the galaxy if you wish, in search of your missing personality components."

"So you knew about that!"

"Of course. I make it my business to know about all of the freaks in my organization. I say to you, Go, Crompton, on your forlorn and hopeless quest. Ten years in stir is too good for you, but it is all that a despicably soft and corrupt judiciary will give you for your larceny, treachery, and bad manners. I want more than that! I want to pay you back more personally. So go, beyond the writ of Terran law. I will find you. My arm is long, my agents many, my revenge secure."

"What are you planning to do to me?" Crompton asked.

"Ah," Blount said, "that would be telling, wouldn't it? Frankly, I'm not quite sure, and I'm in no hurry to make up my mind. There are so many piquant possibilities! I look forward to many pleasant hours of gloating over my plans, anticipating your frenzied and futile struggles, your wretched pleas, and your gasping horrified despair at the end."

"You're sick," Crompton said.

"Not half as sick as you're going to be when I get my hands on you again, Crompton. This I promise you."

Crompton turned and walked away, numbed by the differential juvenescent's hideous yet puerile threat. He presented his ticket to the ticket-tacker, and the ticket-tacker tacked a tick in the ticket's upper right-hand corner and let Crompton pass aboard.

He walked directly into the orange and gray module that ferried passengers to the orbiting spaceship many miles above.

His numbness fell away as the ship soared high into yellow sunlight. Not even the thought of death can upset a man who is going into space for the first time. The journey into the unknown transcends the framework of anxiety, at least for a while.

TWO

7

Aboard the orbiting starship, the passengers fastened their safety belts and sipped from paper cups filled with orange juice. There was an awkward moment when the artificial gravity generator cut out and the hostesses floated into the air, still smiling. But everything was soon under control. Soon the red takeoff light came on.

"This is the voice of your captain, Eddie Remonstrator," said a pleasant Midwestern voice over the public address system. "We are in takeoff configuration now, ladies and gentlemen, and it may be of interest if I describe the procedure, since that is the trickiest part of the whole trip. Now then: the port and starboard searcher probes are extended on full and going through their ninety-degree cycles. As you probably know from magazine articles, these sensors are searching the fabric of space for what are technically called Foster-Harris discontinuity areas, or FHda's for short. These FHda's are like a sort of hole in space, folks, only it might better be compared to a hole through two folds of fabric. You see, space has no substance, but it does have configuration. That was proven by Edkwiser and Braintree back in '09, and it is what makes rapid interstellar flight possible. You must remember, however, that spatial configuration exists only on a single order of magnitude.

"Now, finding a suitable FHda . . . Excuse me a moment, folks. . . . Okay, I'm back now. Our starboard sensor just came up with a fat one, and I'm just about to ease this little old ship right into the FHda helix—because it isn't really a *hole*, folks. It can be best visualized as a hollow tube twisted into a helical shape, and us as going *into* that tube. Spatial configuration always follows helical routes, except in the vicinity of gray stars. That's Von Gresham's Law.

"Okay, we're approaching it now, folks. Soon our ship will be flowing smoothly along the helical path that in n-dimensional space describes a straight line. We're approaching. . . . Ease her to starboard, chief bosun. That's it, steady as she goes. . . . Guide by the flare line along the outer orifice. . . . Just a touch more left rudder. . . . Now meet her, meet her. . . . Steer small, damn you! Trim those cephoid flaps back to zero! Reset the tabulating skin surface totalizer to zero zero niner! Retract the sponge antenna! Give me seven degrees on the bivalvular de-quenching remoulade!" (Here the captain's voice became indistinct, and his words blurry and capable of misinterpretation.) "Okay, now the drumhead marshtide ripcurrent is closing fast! Give me a tune on the fiddle!" (That couldn't be right, Crompton thought: he must have heard wrong.) "Now take a turn around the double avunculars and collapse the spread-fragment tourniquet glide-runners! Watch the dragtimer, it's gaining turbulent spontaneity! There we go! Now trim ballast and it's downhill all the way!"

There was a moment of silence. Then the captain said, "Well, folks, there you are, a blow by blow account of how a starship gets going. We'll be traveling though the FHda helix for some twenty hours of subjective time, so relax and get comfortable. Our hostesses will now be taking orders for psychedelics for those among you who want to space-out while going through space. There is a movie in the forward lounge that sounds mighty good, something about Albert Dekker. Enjoy yourself, folks, this is Captain Eddie Remonstrator signing off."

Crompton rubbed his nose vigorously and wondered whether he was hearing things or if Captain Remonstrator was conducting himself in an unusual manner. Or a little of both, perhaps. . . .

"Yes, actually, it is," the person in the seat next to Crompton remarked.

"What is?" Cromtpon asked.

"A little of both."

"What are you talking about?" Crompton asked.

"I am referring to your last thought before this conversation began. You were wondering if you were hearing things or if Captain Remonstrator was behaving in an unusual manner. Then you thought perhaps it was a little of both, which is the correct answer, and refers to your instinctive understanding of the degree of variability possible on either side of the observer-observed dichotomy."

"So you can read my mind," Crompton said, and looked at the person with attention. He saw a fresh-faced young man with a crew cut, wearing a gray sweater and brown slacks and white buckskin shoes.

"Yes, I can, when I put my mind to it."

"That is an invasion of my privacy," Crompton declared.

"What makes you think so? When you broadcast words, you expect anyone around to hear. Why not when you broadcast thoughts?"

"I want to select the thoughts I broadcast," Crompton said.

"Do you? What a curious attitude. One thought is very much like another, you know. They're just a sort of vibration and there's nothing personal about them. Creatures have been broadcasting words and thoughts at each other for a long time now, and no one is much better or worse for it."

"Aren't you sort of young to be spouting all of this deep stuff?" Crompton asked.

"I am not quite a million years old," the person replied. "On a galactic scale, that's pretty young. Still, I've seen a thing or two in my time."

"I don't find that a very amusing joke," Crompton said.

"I am an Aaian," the young man said. "I always tell the truth, even when I lie. And all Aaian jokes are in bad taste because we're too old to bother being subtle. I see that some proof is called for."

"I should think so," Crompton said.

"Then dig this." The fresh-faced youth reached up and touched his nose. Immediately his face changed to the deeply furrowed mask of an old man. His clothing changed to a tattered gray bathrobe, and his voice rose to a squeaky soprano as he said, "One good metamorphosis is worth a million words."

"Please don't do that," Crompton said, shaken.

The old man changed back into the fresh-faced youth. "Want to see some more demonstrations of my superhuman abilities?"

"I'd rather not," Crompton said. "I believe you. Just give me a little time to adjust."

"Well, really, Crompton," the Aaian said, "if you want to survive out here you're going to have to get on the ball. Some peculiar things happen out beyond Earth, and there's no time for standing around being astonished. Your attitude must be, *Nu*, so strange things happen, so what else is new? Otherwise you're going to malrespond when something really tricky comes along."

Crompton took a deep breath and let it out slowly. He said, "All right, so you're an Aaian and you're a million years old and you have superhuman powers. So what else is new?"

"That's much better. What's new? Well, here you are on a starship and your seatmate turns out to be a member of the race to whose planet you are going. Obviously I know a lot about you. Obviously I've got plans of some sort for you. Obviously you and I are going to have to come to terms with each other."

Crompton nodded. "Obviously. And what else is new?"

"Don't be a wise guy," the Aaian said. "Wouldn't you like to know what this is all about?"

"I'm waiting for you to tell me."

"Crompton, we Aaians are the oldest intelligent race in the galaxy. We're also the smartest. We are immortal, more or less. We've seen it all come down the pike. Long ago we conquered this island universe, but we found it wasn't much good for laughs so we gave it back. There's nothing left for us to do, nothing meaningful in our terms. So we do nothing but play our Game."

"I've heard about the Aaian Game," Crompton said. "But nobody seems to know much about it."

"That's not because we're secretive," the Aaian said. "It's simply that our Game cannot be subsumed under a static description. It can't really be described at all because it is changing constantly, according to rules that we make up as we go along."

"Is that really all you can find to do?" Crompton asked.

The Aaian shrugged. "Ancient and accomplished races have their peculiar problems, Crompton. I mean, after perfect enlightenment, what do you do? You can't expect us to just stand around grinning at each other. So we play our Game. Our idea of a good laugh is to go one up on each other. We are, of course, always aware that each of us is all of us and scoring off another is just the same as scoring off oneself. That's fine with us, because a game should not have a serious outcome. But it should be played hard and fair, and that's what we do according to the rules of the moment."

"That's all very interesting," Crompton said. "But why are you telling me all this?"

"Because you happen to be in my Game, Crompton. Or you will be as soon as this aspect of the Game begins. You are going to be one of the pawns I will manipulate. Doesn't that sound like fun?"

"No, it doesn't," Crompton said. "Count me out."

"Calm down," the Aaian said. "*I* am also one of the pawns *you* are going to manipulate in *your* Game."

"Look, I've got a lot on my mind these days," Crompton said. "I don't have any time for this stuff."

"Recovering your missing personality components and achieving Reintegration are vitally important to you, are they not? They constitute your Game. To succeed, you are going to need my help. Without it, you might as well stay on Earth and do crossword puzzles."

"Specifically," Crompton said, "what do I need your help for?"

"I haven't the slightest idea," the Aaian said. "How can I know anything like that until the Game actually begins?"

"If you can't know that," Crompton said, "how can you know the circumstances will even arise in which I will need your help?"

"Because I *can* know that much," the Aaian said. "After all, I am a being with superhuman powers."

Crompton thought about it, and the more he thought the less he liked what was happening.

"This is all going too fast," he said. "It's not the way I thought things would be."

"Of course not," the Aaian said. "Like most people you want what you want, and only when and how and for as long as you want it. I'm sorry the universe isn't being run according to your requirements, Crompton. But there it is! You can sulk and play hard to get and try to have things your own way and probably get killed before you get to do anything interesting; or you can get with it and maybe we'll both have some fun."

"All right!" Crompton said. "I don't seem to have much choice in the matter! What happens next?"

"Next I tell you my name. It is Secuille. Remember it. We will meet again, later, for the first time, and then we can get right down to business."

"Wait a minute," Crompton said.

"This time doesn't count," Secuille said. "It's completely out of temporal sequence. It's as good as didn't happen."

"Are you telling me that we haven't actually met just now?"

"That's right. Interesting, isn't it? Sometimes it's a bore to let things go along until they actually happen, and these spaceflights are mostly dead time anyhow."

"I don't see," Crompton said, "how we can meet later for the first time when we've met now for the first time."

"But I explained to you," Secuille said, "this meeting doesn't count. I do have to pay a penalty for doing it this way, however: I won't remember any of this when we actually do meet."

"That makes no sense at all."

"Rules never do, do they?" Secuille said. "But there it is. I won't remember you, but you will remember me, and you'll tell me what happened, and I'll catch on quick due to my superlative powers of adaptability, and the Game will begin."

"You may be superhuman," Crompton said, "but I think you're also crazy."

"Well, it looks like it's going to be interesting," Secuille said. "Now I seem to have used up all my lecture material, so I must be off." He smiled at Crompton and vanished.

Crompton sat very still for a while. Then he signaled the hostess.

"Excuse me, miss, could you tell me the name of the young man who was sitting here?"

She said, "You must be joking, sir. That seat has been vacant throughout the flight."

"I was afraid of that," Crompton said.

"Would you like another orange juice?"

"I think I'd better," Crompton said heavily.

8

Traveler, we welcome you to the planet Aaia, and to its capital city, Cetesphe, and to the Hotel Grandspruinge located in the interesting and historic downtown Nevratidae district, and framed in the distance by the stately Oleonian Alps. We have assembled here a few facts for your greater appreciation and enjoyment of our unique civilization.

Aaia, as you perhaps know from *The Guinness Book of Universal Records*, is the oldest planet in the galaxy to be inhabited by a single autochthonous race throughout its history. This rare continuity, plus the fact that Aaia has had no war of any sort for the past 990,000 years, gives this planet an atmosphere of security and down-home coziness not to be equaled elsewhere.

The Aains are a small civilization, limiting themselves to exactly one billion members. They are considered immortal by some, but themselves claim no more than extreme longevity. The oldest living Aaian, Truch Nivera, is *at least* thirteen million years old according to carbon-dating techniques carried out on his toenail parings by the unimpeachable Swiss Bureau of Corroborations. (Mr. Nivera can be seen Friday nights at the Kot Krot Club in West Cetesphe, where he has been giving poetry readings for the last seven hundred years.)

Many people have asked what the Aaians, who have lived so long and experienced so much, do for amusement. This is not an easy question to answer, since Aaians are individualists *par excellence*. Aaians do many different things and learn many curious and useful facts. This is only to be expected of a race that dispensed with fixed personal form two million years ago; a race that consciously chooses its bodies, emotions, values, concepts, etc. In this way Aaians get to live countless lives.

Aaians have no fixed "self" to refer to. Aaians are only who they happen to have chosen to be for a period of time. When the moment comes to be someone or something else, they shed their former bodies, feelings, values, etc., and take on those appropriate to their new roles and existences. From this it may be imagined that the Aaians are bascially a lighthearted race, though races who do not know their ways tend to consider them unreliable in business dealings. (But there is a simple way around this. Before doing any business with an Aaian, ask him for the date of expiration on his current psychosomatic setup. He is bound to honor his commitments during this term by the oldest ethical rule of the race: *Say what you do and do what you say*, in the words of Amirra Tauba, founder of the Aaian Uniform Code of Ethics for Consciously Sentient Beings.)

But getting back to the question of amusement: aside from the multifarious complications which they encounter in their consecutive existences, Aaians are brought together by their devotion to the Game. It is outside the range of this brochure to attempt to characterize the Game. Standard works on the subject are Wolfschmidt's *Players of the Galactic Noh Play* and Charleroi's *Strategy of Incongruity*.

There are many immediate pleasures for the tourist to sample. Of special note is the Gardens of Rui in East Cetesphe. This vast amusement complex, on its own estate of ten million acres of dramatic countryside, borders on the violet waters (made so by the marine organism *grunius*) of the Pyrametique Sea, and commemorates the famous space battle of Inferdung Pass in which the armed forces of Aaia broke the power of the mad Asthark Lethume and his hordes of wild Mitsumian tribesmen. The Gardens are laid out to provide maximum pleasure for each of the space-traveling Nineteen Civilized Species. There is much here for everyone, and at modest cost. For the adventurous, there are pleasures compounded of the most guilty and deeply hidden desires—to be brought to light and staged for you by a plentiful staff of your own species to ensure the authenticity of all delights—unlike the Gouville FunLand on Drog'hvasta II, where all services, sexual and otherwise, are performed by shape-changing (and sometimes absentminded!) Duverian Hungorfyyords.

But the description is not the described, as Amirra Tauba remarked as he chewed up the map of the galaxy! Words, in the final analysis, are just about as futile as actions, and much less fun. So welcome to Aaia, where we promise you the time of your incarnation!

Crompton put the brochure in his pocket. He was sitting in the lobby of the Pingala Arms in downtown Cetesphe. His ship had "come out of the tube" (as Captain Remonstrator jocularly expressed it) some twelve hours previously. He was now seated in the lobby of his hotel awaiting the arrival of a man who might be able to help him.

Edgar Loomis, whom he sought, was the pleasure component of the scattered Crompton personality. He was the fun-seeker, the sensation-lover; without him, there was no party for Crompton, no immediacy, no Now. Loomis was indispensable. But it looked as though there were going to be considerable difficulties in finding him.

Soon after his arrival, Crompton had gone to the Hall of Records, where information on the whereabouts of all beings on Aaia was scrupulously maintained and updated. He was told that Edgar Loomis was in good health and was currently employed at the Gardens of Rui. But no other information was given to him: by virtue of a very recent law, the addresses of persons and other beings working in the Gardens were no longer to be disclosed. The android clerk, though sympathetic and in agreement that the law made no apparent sense, could do nothing for him except suggest that he conduct a personal search of the Gardens.

Crompton decided against this. It would be futile, considering their vast extent and the hordes of people employed there, some of them indoors in capacities that would make a chance encounter with a male of their own race unlikely in the extreme.

He discussed his problem with the desk clerk at the Pingala Arms. The clerk hinted that something might be done, under certain circumstances difficult to define. Crompton, after several agonizing seconds, figured out what the man meant and, crimson with embarrassment, offered him a crumpled handful of Aaian pronics. The clerk accepted them matter-of-factly and made a telegnomic call. He told Crompton to wait in the lobby until someone came for him.

The hotel's central intake orifice dilated and a small hunchbacked person in a long tattered gray overcoat and cracked brown shoes slid through and said, "You Crompton? Follow me."

He led Crompton outside, to a waiting limousine. (Crompton learned later that this vehicle ran on the power supplied by a small psychophysical converter that extracted volition from chimpanzees bred especially for this purpose, then converted that energy into torque.) The hunchback seated himself next to Crompton and waited until Crompton paid him six hundred pronics. Then he gave instructions to the driver and the vehicle gibbered away.

The hunchback said, "I'm not guaranteeing anything,

but I'm taking you to see the only person who can help you, if he wants to."

"Who is this person?" Crompton asked.

"He is the newly elected Council Member for East Cetesphe. He is also the person who sponsored the law that prevents you from learning what you need to know."

"How can he help me?"

"It is a custom of Aaia that the man responsible for a new law is also granted a legal exception to that law, to use as he pleases, or to bestow on someone else."

"You're saying that the man who passes a new law is legally entitled to break it?"

"Precisely."

"But that's immoral! It's blatant corruption!"

"On the contrary, the law prevents corruption by legitimatizing it."

"That makes no sense to me at all," Crompton said. "And anyhow, why would this Council Member want to help me?"

"For the same reason that the desk clerk and I are helping you," the hunchback said. "For a bribe."

"I see," Crompton said coldly.

"We're very much into bribery this century," the hunchback explained. "It's become quite a fad."

Crompton sat in scornful silence.

"I suppose you were expecting more godlike behavior?"

"Well—"

"Most tourists do. But we Aaians got sick of the godlike thing many thousands of years ago. It wasn't much fun, and it interfered with the Game."

"I see," Crompton said.

They rode in silence for a while. Then the hunchback said, "I see that you're wondering how come I, an Aaian with the power to take on any shape I desire, am currently walking around with a hunchback and tatty clothes."

"I really don't like you reading my mind," Crompton snapped.

"Sorry," the Aaian said.

After a while Crompton asked, "Well, since you brought it up, why?"

"It's because of a bad move I made in the Game a few centuries ago. I've got to wear this body exactly as it is for another eighty years. The hunch isn't so bad—I can store water in it, you know—but I've got dyspepsia so bad it would drive you crazy."

"Huh," Crompton said.

"You're really not a very interesting conversationalist," the hunchback told him. "Anyhow, here we are." The car came to a stop in front of a small green office building. "Go right down the central corridor and enter the first door on your right. Good luck."

Crompton got out. The car gibbered away, and Crompton entered the office building. He found the door that the hunchback had indicated. He knocked.

"Come in," a voice said.

Crompton opened the door and walked into a richly furnished office. At a desk, turning toward him now, was an Aaian with a familiar face and an unmistakable crew cut. It was Secuille.

9

Secuille looked at him as though seeing him for the first time. "Yes, what can I do for you?" he asked in a pleasant, slightly harassed voice.

"I'm Alistair Crompton. Don't you remember me?"

Secuille studied his face, then shook his head. "I'm afraid not. Perhaps you've mixed me up with someone else."

"Your name is Secuille," Crompton said. "We just met on a starship. We talked for about an hour, then you disappeared."

"You're quite sure of that?"

"It's not the sort of thing I'd be likely to get wrong. You told me that you were playing the Game, or just about to begin playing it. You said that I was going to be a pawn in your Game."

"Damnation!" Secuille struck his forehead with the flat of his hand. "Wait a minute," he said. "I'm going to check this out with Giant Computer."

He pressed a button on a small violet tabletop computer terminal situated just to the left of the blotter. He asked, "Did I happen to commit myself to the Game in the last few days? And was I out of temporal sequence for a part of that time?" He studied the flashing lights on the readout panel, then said, "I see. Thank you, Giant Computer." He turned to Crompton. "What else did I tell you?"

"You said that you thought it might be amusing to explain things to me out of temporal sequence. You said that you wouldn't remember, however, and I would have to remind you."

"I see," Secuille said. "Yes, it's just the sort of clownish stunt I'm likely to do. There was this party last week, and some pretty potent items were passed around. We Aaians take anything, you know, because we can't be killed that way; maybe *no* way, but certainly not that way. So we drop it all down the old hatch, whatever it is. We've been doing this for untold millennia, and it takes quite a lot to get us off. Most of the time we just get a bad taste in the mouth. So when Chush and his twin brought the packet of semi-aspirated derii weed from Aztec II, I thought nothing of it. The next two days were a blank. I wish I could get some more of that stuff. . . ."

"I don't understand any of this," Crompton said. "But I *do* have my own problems. Will you give me the address of Edgar Loomis?"

"And who," Secuille asked, "is Edgar Loomis?"

"Must I go through all of that again?" Crompton asked. "You said on the ship that by meeting me out of temporal sequence we could cut out the tedious explanations when we actually did meet, which I presume is now, unless this meeting also doesn't count."

"Calm down," Secuille said. "I've just taken the liberty of peeking into your mind and finding out about Edgar Loomis and all the rest of it. I'm completely at home with the situation now. By the way, I'm sorry I passed that law concerning the employees of the Rui Gardens. I had no idea it would affect you."

"It's quite obvious that you did that," Crompton said, "in order to force me to find you and ask a favor."

"It's not as simple as that," Secuille said. "I—the identity who is speaking to you now—had no idea of your existence, and passed the nondisclosure law in all innocence. It was one of my other identities, the one whom you met on the starship, who influenced me to pass that law."

"How many identities do you have?" Crompton asked.

"Innumerable," Secuille said.

"I find all of this difficult to believe," Crompton said.

"That is only because you haven't consciously experienced for yourself the influences which your selves, past and present, have on the identity you happen to be at the moment. Crompton, every sentient creature lives simultaneously in various timebound sequences, and tries to better things for himself by influencing one or more of his other selves. The voices that you hear in your head, telling you what to do and what not to do, these are the voices of your other selves at other times and places, casting their votes, trying to improve conditions for themselves."

"Maybe that's true for you," Crompton said. "But it's not for me. I'm always the same person."

"Some of your other selves are presently out of touch," Secuille admitted. "But what I say is as true for you as it is for me. You yourself, at this moment, are nothing more than one thin voice in the mind of some inconceivable Crompton who might not yet have dreamed that this was one of his situations."

"I don't understand any of that," Crompton said. "The fact remains that you passed the law that won't allow me to learn Loomis's whereabouts. And now I suppose you'll give me his address only if I agree to be a pawn in your Game."

Secuille looked amazed, then threw back his head and laughed. Aaians don't laugh whole-heartedly as a rule when in the company of other beings: Aaians, being ancient and wise, are filled to bursting with various kinds of psychic powers. The sudden explosive release of emotion tends to allow these powers to manifest.

That is what happened now. Secuille's laughter gave form to the following beings: a brown-skinned girl with long black hair and dancing dark eyes, two Babylonian demons, a yeti, and a red-faced man in a brown and yellow checked suit.

"Do you see what I see?" one of the demons remarked to the other, indicating the girl. "Poontang!"

"Is good to eat?" the other demon asked.

"Eeee," said the girl.

"To think," said the red-faced man, "that I should wind up to be mere illusion in the mind of an extraterrestrial being who, during my lifetime, I never even dreamed existed! Yet he might equally be a figment of someone else's imagination. Which would make me an apparition of a second order of unreality, counting from the left."

"Let's get married," the brown-skinned girl said to no one in particular.

"All right, that's enough of that," Secuille said; and the illusions forlornly turned into smoke and reentered the Aaian's head, all except the yeti, who escaped by the fire exit and was hunted down and dispatched several days later by the Royal Aaian Illusion Squad.

"You have really missed the point, Crompton," Secuille said after everything was back under control and the chair that the yeti had knocked over had set itself upright, somewhat abashed at having been overturned by a mere illusion. "Can you actually believe that I would try to coerce you into playing in my Game?"

"Well, you'll have to admit that it does look that way."

"Maybe it does to you," Secuille said, "but not to me. To me it looks like the long arm of synchronicity is stirring things into patterns again. Mr. Loomis's address is 4567 Panderer Way, South Palmetto Shores, West Garden, South Cetesphe. He works daily at the Episodes Division of Pleasure Scenes Galaxy Spectaculars in the Gardens of Rui."

Crompton was stunned. After a while he muttered, "Thank you very much."

"You're entirely welcome," Secuille said.

"And what happens now?"

"What do you mean?"

"You've done me a big favor. What do I have to do for you in return?"

"Just stay as sweet as you are," Secuille said.

"But I thought you needed me in your Game!"

"That's not important," Secuille said.

"I never said that I would not help you," Crompton said. "It's just that the way it came up—"

Secuille led him gently to the door. "Good-bye, Crompton. It may be that we will meet again under different conditions. Feel free to call on me for assistance. And, as much as one temporary combination of bound energies can wish another good luck, I do so wish you."

He closed the door. And Crompton, feeling completely one-upped, walked out into the disconsolate night.

10

Crompton took a jitney ornithopter to the Episodes Division of Pleasure Scenes Galaxy Spectaculars in the Gardens of Rui. This part of the Gardens was devoted to the needs of humanoform beings and their near-relatives. These included the humans, the alinopods, the gnoles, the subquasfian tadies, the barbizans of Grustark II, the irrepressible double-jointed trelizonds, the insidious and falsely smiling lunters, and their neighbors, the hyperpromenteian muns.

As Crompton passed through the main gate, he saw a lean, intense-looking man in blue jeans and black-rimmed spectacles sitting on a stool and working away at a portable typewriter on his lap. Crompton stared at him with amazement, and the man looked up and said, "Yes, what is it?"

"I'd like to know what you're doing," Crompton asked.

"I'm writing a novel," the man said, typing as he talked. "This dialogue goes in, of course. My detractors accuse me of mere fantasizing, but I put in only what I see and hear."

"It seems to me—"

"Never mind," the writer said. "No line of dialogue beginning 'It seems to me' ever turns out to be amusing. Perhaps I should deliver a set speech at this point. There are several delicious ironies that perhaps have not occurred to you to date. For example—"

"I hate sentences that begin 'For example,'" Crompton said.

"I was going to rewrite that, actually. 'Do I contradict myself? Very well, then, I contradict myself—I am large. I contain multitudes.' How well old Whitman put it! The peculiar relevance of that conception—"

"I must be going," Crompton said.

"Good-bye," the writer said. "It's been a short scene, but a snappy one."

"It must be nice being a writer," Crompton said.

"It is like being a slug crawling down an infinite sheet of paper."

"That's too bad," Crompton said. "Maybe—"

But the writer never listened to sentences that began "Maybe." His attention had already been captured by the sudden entrance of a fat man clutching the leaden effigy of a black bird to his chest, closely followed by Humphrey Bogart, Mary Astor, Peter Lorre, and—in a surprise cameo appearance—Albert Dekker! "This is more like it!" the writer said, and proceeded to type furiously while smoking two cigarettes.

Crompton ambled on. The setting for the Episodes Division was a long, rather indistinct street in an unknown city. As visitors walked along, looking for amusement, fragments of conversation and bits of action unrolled with pleasing ambiguity. They could walk on and see what the next episode would bring, or stop wherever they pleased and take part in the unfolding situation.

Matters didn't actually work out that well, due to irreconcilable nomenclatural and procedural differences caused by the crowded presence and divergent demands of various humanoform but mutually unviable races. The producers of

Episodes welcomed the resultant dense ambiguous proximities while deploring them publicly; for nearness and strangeness forever lure the curious despite their pious protestations. And that means money, a commodity that the Aaians had arbitrarily decided to value for a few centuries just to see if there was anything in it.

As Crompton walked along, he heard a double-jointed and irrepressible trelizond in full autumn plumage remark to its three brothers, "I'm leaving for Funthris today, may my place in the nest fall vacant!" Nearby, a pride of gnoles were tickling a subquasfian tadie into paroxysms, while chanting, "We Move Unmoved through Moving Moves," to the consternation of the silent alinopod in the tree. Close to them, one human female was saying to another, "I don't know who could help you with a problem like that, Josie." Nearby, seven muns were trying to engage in sexual psillicosis by parentian closure—rather pathetically, since they lacked the all-important badminton equipment. There were more ominous matters happening nearby, where a barbizan in leaf mail and pointed olymphat was tapping a message of disillusion on the thorax and subabdominal feelers of an insidious and falsely smiling lunter, caught red-handed in the illicit and impossible act of surrogate transformation.

None of these scenes caught Crompton's fancy, of course. Each was intended to titillate the senses of a particular deviant of a particular humanoform—but not necessarily human—species. Most of what these creatures were doing to one another was incomprehensible to Crompton, just as what humans do to each other is meaningless to other humanoforms. This is the situation of ultimate reciprocal bewilderment, and it renders our own vaunted incomprehension of ourselves and our fellow man as pretty small potatoes indeed.

Crompton was reduced to staring around him, bewildered, a disembodied intelligence floating through scenes from some surrealistic hell, as this pageant of creatures acted out exotic emotions representative of their indescribable realities.

It was senseless for him to continue in this way. He turned back, pushing past two tadies tap-dancing on the broad, shovel-shaped nose of a molting barbizan, and other, even less savory sights, until he came to the main gate and the typewriting writer.

"You seem to know a lot," Crompton said to him. "Maybe you could tell me where I'd find Edgar Loomis?"

"You've come to the right man," the writer said, turning on his cassette recorder and lighting a third cigarette. "I am acting as my own *deus ex machina*, you know, so it will do no disservice to the formal elegance of my scheme if I tell you that Mr. Loomis is in the fourth scene to your left, and his drama is even now ending. I fear you must hurry, my friend. But before you go, let me say a word or two about your overall situation." There followed a ten-minute lecture on various nuances and subtleties that Crompton had almost certainly overlooked in his appraisal of where it was all at. During this time Crompton stood motionless, not even blinking, due to the small paralysis gun in whose beam he was frozen. This instrument was standard issue to members of the Galactic Writers Guild, and was designed to ensure the respect and attention of unappreciative audiences during the dull but meaningful parts.

At length the writer concluded with a quotation from Rilke and turned off the paralysis gun. "And now," he said, "let's hear a nice round of applause, plus the Guild minimum fee of one hundred prontics for a nonexclusive one-shot hearing of an impromptu passage of moral import."

"Like hell," Crompton growled.

"Pay," the writer said sternly, "or I shall be forced to turn on the paralysis beam again and give you a ten-minute lecture on Gratitude at standard rates."

Crompton paid, applauded perfunctorily, and rushed off.

He reached the designated place just in time to see a bearded man in a dhoti declare to the audience: "And so on sweet Antione's tombstone it shall be duly graven: 'She never saw it coming!' "

The audience—thirty-seven middle-aged and jovial people from Phoenix, Arizona—really broke up at that one.

The bearded man bowed and vanished.

Crompton grabbed one of the audience—John Winslow Audience from Flagstaff, by an eerie coincidence—and demanded, "The actors! Where did they go?"

John Audience—a portly, jovial man with steely blue

eyes and an incongruous dueling scar on his left cheek—pulled his arm free peremptorily.

"What did you say?" he demanded.

"I said, 'The actors, where did they go?' "

"Oh, I guess they went backstage to get ready for the grand finale, which will be starting any moment now," the man said helpfully.

"Was one of the actors named Edgar Loomis?"

"I believe I saw that name on the program," Audience said, his hard blue eyes becoming momentarily gelid. "Yes, by jingo; Loomis, he was one of the actors."

"What did he look like?"

"He had on a silver shirt."

"Is that all you remember?"

"It was the most distinguishing thing about him. You'll be able to see him in the finale. Look, it's beginning!"

A large stage had appeared. Crowded on it were all of the humanoforms who had performed in that night's episodes. Behind them were two symphony orchestras. As Crompton watched, all of these beings threw off their clothing and crowded together, closer, closer, writhing and slipping and sliding over, around, under, and into each other in an unlikely potpourri of arms, thoraxes, feelers, wings, cunts, chitins, claws, tentacles, cocks, shoulders, heads, ovipositors, exoskeletons, pistils, kneecaps, mandibles, fins, stamens, suckers, and the like. Somehow, despite their contorted and unnatural positions, the humanoforms were able to sing, squeak, whistle, and vibrate the following song:

> People and gnoles and hingers and tadies,
> Barbizans, trelizonds, lunters, and muns
> All in together in sexual friendliness—
> Love conquers all, even beastly fat gruns!

A beastly fat gruns now appeared at the top of the quivering mound of flesh, chitin, et cetera. The gruns was grinning! It was a first for the Gardens of Rui!

The audience—sentimentalists all—applauded wildly. Trumpets blared, and a long roll of kettledrums began. The audience watched with bated breath as the great mound of composite flesh, chitins, et cetera, heaved and strained, grunted and groaned, strove and endeavored. . . .

Crompton caught a glimpse of a silver elbow down near the bottom left-hand corner of the stack. Loomis! It had to be Loomis!

And then the entire great mound of intermingled and interpenetrated humanoforms came simultaneously in a vast greenish white orgasm of various forcibly expelled secretions. The audience really lapped it up, but Crompton, revolted, was already on his way toward the exit, heading as quickly as possible for his hotel room and a game of solitaire.

11

Crompton had not been prepared for the squalid depravity of Loomis's employ. Now, sitting in the curtained quiet of his hotel room, he was filled with doubts. It had occurred to him to wonder whether he actually wanted a creature like Loomis taking up room in his mind.

Loomis was going to be trouble. He really didn't want him around. But unfortunately, he had to have him. Reintegration was impossible without all of the original components.

But perhaps it would not be so bad. Dan Stack, the third component of Crompton's mind, would doubtless serve as an equipoise to Loomis's base impulses, once he was found and assimilated. And Loomis himself might be expected to show some gratitude for this rescue from his pointless and repetitive existence. If the man possessed the slightest bit of moral rectitude, he might be expected to keep himself under restraint until such time as his qualities had been assimilated into the new and integrated personality that Crompton was planning to become.

Encouraged by this line of thought, Crompton put away his cards and straightened up his room. With set jaw and determined eye, he straightened his tie and went out into the street.

He boarded a cruising ornithopter and gave its driver Loomis's home address. He was not interested in the alien sights on all sides of him, sights which *Playboy* magazine had voted "Most Far-out in the Galaxy" for three consecutive years. The ornithopter flapped to a graceful landing on the front lawn of the aluminum-sided ranch house with carport, jalousies, a Florida room, a swimming pool, and a hibiscus tree. Crompton paid the driver (a freckled CCNY student on a working vacation). Trying to maintain his composure, he went up to the front door and rang the chimes.

The door opened. A girl of about five in a soiled T-shirt looked up at him. "Whaddaya want?"

"Ah—is Mr. Loomis in?"

"What do you want him for?"

"That is a personal matter," Crompton said.

"I don't like you," the child said.

"Gwendkwifer," a woman's voice called from behind the child. "Come here, please."

The little girl went away. A dark and boldly attractive young woman looked out at Crompton. "Who are you?"

"My name is Crompton. I am here to see Mr. Loomis on a matter of considerable importance to both of us."

"If you're a bill collector, forget it, he's broke."

"It is nothing like that," Crompton said.

A man's voice from within the house said, "Get out of the way, Gilliam. I can handle this."

The door opened. Mr. Loomis looked out at Mr. Crompton.

Tableau!

Parts of the same personality recognize each other instantly, and through any disguise. The moment is always the same, almost sickening in its intensity, a moment so paradoxically and simultaneously attractive and repulsive that response is momentarily arrested while one tries to

think of something to say. For what *do* you say after the
initial shock has worn off? Should you take an informal
line? ("Hello, missing personality-segment, always glad to
see a part of myself, come in and take your shoes off. . . .")
Or is it a time for caution? ("Oh, *you*'ve popped up again.
I do hope you'll watch your manners this time. . . .")

So it was that these two fragments of a single personality gazed upon each other without speaking. Crompton
saw the signs of a decaying Durier body. He observed
Loomis's neat, handsome features, somewhat blurry now,
characterologically gone to fat. He noticed the smooth,
thinning brown hair artfully cut, and the brilliant eyes
around which was a trace of cosmetics. And you could depend on Crompton not to overlook the self-indulgent twist
to Loomis's mouth and the complacent slouch of his body.

Here was the stereotype of the Sensualist, the man
who lives only for pleasure and slothful ease. Here was the
embodiment of the Sanguine Humor of Fire, caused by too
much hot blood, tending to make a man unduly mirthful
and overfond of fleshy gratifications. In Loomis resided all
of Crompton's potentialities for pleasure, untimely ripped
from him and set up as an entity in itself—Loomis, the
pure pleasure principle, vitally necessary to the Crompton
mind body.

This pleasure principle, which Crompton had always
imagined as existing *in vacuo,* seemed to be endowed with
a personality of its own, to say nothing of the unexpected
complication of a wife and child.

"Well well well," Loomis said, grinning and rocking
on his heels. "I always figured you'd look me up one of
these days."

"Who is this creep?" Gilliam asked. (The actual word
she used was *nmezpelth,* a bit of Trastanian slang she had
picked up from her far-traveling tap-dancing father.
Nmezpelth means "diseased slime-mold" and carries the
connotation of "dismal repetition of undesirable actions.")

"He is my only living relative," Loomis said.

Gilliam peered suspiciously at Crompton. "Is he a second cousin or something?"

"Afraid not," Loomis said. "Biologically he is a sort of
combination brother and father to me. I don't believe
there's a word to describe the relationship."

"You told me you were an orphan!"

Loomis shrugged. "Well, you told me you were a virgin."

"You bastard! What is this all about?"

Loomis said, "Oh well, these things always come out in the end, don't they? Gilliam, I have a confession to make. The fact is, I'm not actually a person at all. I am no more than a portion of this person's personality."

"That's really funny," Gilliam said, laughing unpleasantly. "You're always bragging about how big a man you are, and now I find out you're not even a man at all."

Loomis smiled. "My dear, you couldn't even satisfy a Durian android; God help us both if I'd been a man!"

"Now *that*," Gilliam said, her voice rising to a scream, "is just too damn much! Baby, I'm splitting because *you* are not where it's at."

"Go back to the job where I found you. What was it—graveyard-shift waitress at the Last Chance Simulacrum Café? Doubtless that is more your speed."

"I'm going!" Gilliam shouted. "I'll send for my clothes! You'll hear from my lawyer!"

She scooped up Gwendkwifer, who screamed, "I don't want to go! I want to see what happens next to Daddy!"

"Precocious little thing," Loomis remarked to Crompton. "Good-bye, my dears," he said, as Gilliam and Gwendkwifer exited.

12

"Well, alone at last," Loomis said, bolting the door. He looked Crompton up and down and didn't seem too pleased with what he saw. "Did you have a pleasant trip here, Alistair? And do you expect to stay long?"

"That depends," Crompton said.

"Well, come into my parlor and let's have a gab."

Loomis's parlor was a wonder and a revelation. Crompton almost stumbled as his feet sank into the deep-piled Oriental rug. The lighting in the room was dim and golden, and a succession of faint and disturbing shadows writhed and twisted across the walls, coiling and closing, transmuting into animals and the blotchy forms of children's nightmares, and disappearing into the mosaic ceiling. Crompton had heard of shadow songs, but had never before seen one.

Loomis said, "It's playing a rather fragile little piece called 'Descent to Xanadu.' How do you like it?"

Crompton shrugged. "It must have been very expensive."

Loomis shrugged. "I wouldn't know. It was a gift. Won't you sit down?"

Crompton settled into a deep armchair that conformed to his contours and began, very gently, to massage his back.

"Something to drink?" Loomis asked.

"Depolymerized sarsaparilla, if you have it," Crompton said.

Loomis went to get drinks. Crompton heard a melody

that seemed to originate in his own head. The tune was slow and sensuous, and unbearably poignant. It seemed to Crompton that he had heard it before, in another time and place.

"It's called 'Terminal Freedom,' " Loomis said, returning. "Direct aural transmission. Pleasant little thing, isn't it?"

Crompton knew that Loomis was trying to impress him. And he *was* impressed. As Loomis poured drinks, Crompton looked around the room at the sculptures, drapes, furniture, gadgets; his clerky mind made some estimates. The goods in this room had cost a great deal of money.

Crompton sipped his drink. It was an Aaian concoction; a feeling of well-being began to pervade him. He said reluctantly, "Pretty good."

He didn't expect Loomis to possess such a measure of composure; or, as they say in the crosswords, *sang-froid*. It disturbed him. Loomis's obvious competence, ease, and command of the situation argued the disturbing idea that perhaps Loomis was not as inadequate a personality as represented. If that were so, where did it leave Crompton? Middle or low man on the personality dominance totem pole? But that simply could not be. To have come all this way to have a mere sensualist dominate him? No!

"I have come here," Crompton said, "for the purpose of effecting Reintegration, which, as I'm sure you know, is our legal and moral prerogative."

"Come to dissolve me back into your personality, eh, Alistair?" Loomis said merrily.

"The goal," Crompton pointed out, "is a state of fusion in which our various factors combine to form a new person, one which will partake of each of our memories equally, and so equally be each of us."

"That's what is supposed to happen," Loomis said. "Personally, I have my doubts. And why should I run the risk of finding out? I'm perfectly happy just the way I am."

"Happiness is impossible for an inadequate and truncated personality such as yourself," Crompton said.

"Well, just between us, I know what you mean. A life devoted exclusively to pleasure with no regard for higher values is a dog's life. It's a fact. Desires fade, Alistair, yet I continue the same weary round of repetitions. No, pleasure is not the fun it's cracked up to be."

"Well then——"

"But pleasure is the only game in town. Basically, I'm a party person, Al, not a deep thinker. Sure, pleasure isn't all fun, but who am I to complain about it? It's a living, isn't it? A man must do his work, even if his work happens to be the pursuit of pleasures he no longer cares about. That's what being a man means."

"I don't think that definition would stand up to any real examination," Crompton said.

"Precisely why I will not give it one," Loomis said. "My motto is: Be courageous, follow your impulses, and ignore the obvious!"

"Have you always lived by that motto?" Crompton asked.

"I guess I always have. I always knew I was different from others. But it didn't bother me much as a kid. I was always popular in school. Not much on education, of course; or not on the education they thought they were teaching me. But I picked up a lot on my own. What treasures of sensuality existed for me in those days! Early adolescence is a beautiful time. But you know how children are—a lot of fooling around, but not much of the real thing. The real thing began for me with Miss Tristana de Cunha, my history teacher. She was a tall woman in her late twenties. Beneath her shapeless schoolmarm clothing she had the body of a nymph! She was an inexhaustible treasure of sensuality. And after her there was Clovis, then Jennifer . . ."

"How long did you continue your formal education?" Crompton asked.

"I dropped out at the age of sixteen. Or rather, I was invited to leave. I was accused of corrupting minors (though only a minor myself!). They said that I was staging 'unspeakable orgies.' A gross exaggeration, I can assure you. In any event, formal education held no charm for me. I was young, attractive, energetic, enthusiastic, and I knew even then what I wanted to be in life."

"What was that?"

"I wanted to be a lifeguard at the Aaia Country Club. I've always envied and admired lifeguards. They get all the action. It's such a beautiful job. There you are, all alone above the crowd, wearing nothing but trunks, sandals, and a white pith helmet. And of course you've got a shiny brass whistle around your neck! Naturally you get a fantastic tan. And the action? A lifeguard is a seminaked authority figure as well as a symbol of summer sensuality. I attained that job in my seventeenth year, after working as busboy and waiter. It was really fantastic."

"What happened?"

"One of those things. One day, after I held the job for two years, there was an emergency. Somebody was in trouble out beyond the marker buoys. I got in my boat and rowed out. It was a very fat woman from Earth. I tried to get her into the boat, but she panicked and capsized me. I struggled with her, trying to tow her to the overturned boat, begging her to keep still while I got us back to shore. But she was out of her head crazy with hysteria and she had a stranglehold around my neck. I realized that the only thing I could do was clip her one on the jaw and tow her in like a stranded whale. Before I could do that, however, *she* clipped *me*—a round-house right with her three hundred-odd pounds of berserk strength behind it. I went out like a light. Luckily, people had noticed my difficulties and sent out another boat. It was just one of those things that could happen to anybody."

"But the management didn't see it that way?"

"They accused me of not knowing how to swim! If you can believe that! Me, who had been their lifeguard for two years!"

"Surely you could prove to them your competence in that department?"

"Frankly, I wouldn't lower myself to it. If that was what they thought of me, to hell with them. I resigned my position."

"What did you do then?" Crompton asked.

"I considered my situation."

"For how long?"

"About a year."

"How did you live during that time?"

"Fortunately I had a sponsor—Miss Suzy Gretsch. That was the woman who had cost me my job. She was grateful to me for having saved her life—"

"But you hadn't saved her life!"

"In her opinion, I had. She was a generous woman,

with a certain flair for sexuality belied by her ungainly body. She was the first person to find artistic talent in me, and to wish to develop it."

"What artistic talent did she find?"

"I've always had a facility for sketching quick caricatures. She made me see that I had serious talent there, one worthy of development. Under her sponsorship I enrolled in art school."

"You were living with her at the time?"

"Of course. She was so lonely, poor thing. It was the least I could do for her. And it was really quite pleasant. I gave that woman the best time she ever had in her life. The small sums that I required for my clothing and odds and ends were nothing to her. We were quite devoted to each other. She even wanted to marry me."

"So what happened?"

"Poor Suzy! She became pathologically, irrationally jealous."

"Why?"

"She had the silly suspicion that I was playing around with the models at art class."

"Were you?"

"Well, of course. But I was doing it all so cleverly that she could never find out a thing. And since she had no real evidence, her jealousy was irrational. All might still have been well if she hadn't hired that detective. He couldn't find anything really incriminating, either; but to save his reputation, he framed me. He bribed three models to swear that they had had relationships with me, singly, *ensemble*, and with others. The damnable thing was that it was true, but he hadn't caught me at it. Still, the technical fact of it having actually happened prevented me from showing Suzy that I had been framed. . . . It resulted in quite a nasty scene, as you can imagine. I gave her back her ankle bracelet and left her apartment."

Things were never quite so good for Loomis after the lifeguard job. He did manage to get hired as a substitute bartender at one of the popular nightclubs. It was a good situation: bartenders have first crack at the female customers, also an inside track with the waitresses. He really wanted to hold on to this one. And he did well at it. But—

"I got fired," he admitted candidly. "It was because

Leela made a scene and the owner decided that I was trouble. I'd been living with Leela for about a month at that time. Leela wasn't her real name. She'd picked that up from some book. She started these scenes because Myra, whom I had recently met, was always hanging around. As if I could stop her from coming into the bar!"

"Why was she always hanging around?"

"Well, she'd become dependent on me. Foolishly enough, I had agreed to help her out. She was learning to be an exotic dancer, and she needed someone with sure hands to hold her while she practiced splits and backbends. Leela put the worst possible interpretation on this, of course."

"Did she have cause?" Crompton asked.

Loomis shook his head impatiently. "She never caught me doing anything out of line with Myra. So why should she be so certain? What right did she have to make a big public mess, and to accuse me—with no evidence at all—of sleeping with Myra and Bunny? Any court anywhere in the galaxy would exonerate me—"

"Wait a minute. Who was Bunny?"

"Bunny was Myra's sister. About sixteen, a charming little thing with great blue eyes and a cute, immature little figure."

"And what were you doing with her?"

"Only what I had to do."

"What are you talking about?"

"You see, they lived together in a one-room efficiency. Bunny began to get ideas. And Myra didn't care. That Myra!"

"So Leela made a scene and that was the end of your job?"

"That's right. My life became a succession of temporary jobs and temporary women. One of those women was Gilliam. And that brings us up to date."

"What made you decide to marry Gilliam?"

"Well, she insisted. She was the only one who ever really insisted. That's love, isn't it? And she was pretty good-looking, and rich. I figured, how far wrong can I go? It just goes to show you, doesn't it?"

"Is Gilliam rich? I thought you said she worked as a waitress."

"She was just doing it for a goof. For a while I

thought we could be happy together—just her and me and her money. But it was not to be. We've had our problems."

"Other women?"

"What else? I seem to be cursed with this powerful interest in women."

"In their sexuality, you mean," Crompton stated.

"Well, of course. That's what women want men to be interested in them for, Alistair. Women *are* their sexual natures. Very few men are aware of this."

"That surely isn't true," Crompton said. "From what I've seen, nearly all men are interested in sex."

"It's not the same thing," Loomis said. "Being interested in sex is simply being interested in one's own sensations. But few men are interested in women's sexual nature. It frightens them. You're a virgin, Al, aren't you?"

"We are discussing you, not me. If I understand correctly, you live off the earnings of women."

"And we all know what *that* is," Loomis said. "Don't be so high and mighty, Alistair! Men and women *do* live off each other—all except the freaks like you."

"You are a mere parasite of the wealthy," Crompton said.

"Now that's really unfair," Loomis said. "Don't the rich have their necessities, too? Maybe they don't need the same things as the poor, but they do have needs. The government provides food, shelter, and medical attention for the poor. But what do they do for the rich?"

Crompton laughed. A short, unpleasant sound. "If anyone finds it a hardship to be rich, he is free to give up the burden."

"But nobody can do that! The poor are stuck with their poverty, and the rich are saddled with their wealth. That's life, it simply can't be helped. The rich need sympathy; and I am very sympathetic to their problems. They need people around them who can enjoy and appreciate luxuries, and teach *them* how to enjoy them as well. I perform that function, making it more possible for them to enjoy their lot in life. And rich women, Alistair! They have their needs, too. They are nervous, highly bred, suspicious, these women, and highly suggestible. They need nuance and subtlety. They need the attentions of a man of soaring imagination, yet possessed of an exquisite sensibility. Such men are all too rare in this humdrum world. Fortunately enough, my own talents lie in that direction."

Crompton stared at Loomis with a certain horror. He found it difficult to believe that this corrupt, self-satisfied seducer was a part of him, a potentiality of his own psyche. He would have been glad to turn away from Loomis and avoid the whole distasteful business of sex. But it could not be: an inscrutable destiny had proclaimed that even the most lucid and clearest-thinking men must still live with that debased aspect of themselves, must come to terms (by sublimation, if possible!) with the shameful male instinct to fuck a lot of women and have a lot of laughs and get paid a lot of money for doing nothing.

It was regrettable, but he had to have Loomis. And perhaps it wouldn't be so bad. Crompton had no doubt of his ability to keep an impulsive, changeable, impulse-ruled creature like that in line, maybe even help him to transform his useless rutting instinct into a passion for architecture or a love of gardening, or something like that.

"All of that is really of no concern to me," Crompton said. "As you know, I am the basic Crompton personality in the original Crompton body. I have come here to Aaia to effect Reintegration with you. I suppose you'll want some time in which to put your affairs in order?"

"My affairs are always in order," Loomis said. "I just take up with whoever wants to get it on with me."

"I meant business matters, such as outstanding debts you might wish to liquidate, settlement of property, and so on."

"I usually don't concern myself too much about that sort of thing," Loomis said. "I figure that taking care of the mess I leave behind after I'm gone is someone else's business, if you see what I mean."

"As you wish. Shall we get on with it?"

"I beg your pardon?"

"With the fusion!"

"Oh, yeah," Loomis said. "That's the part I'm kinda doubtful about." He thought for a moment. "I've been thinking about it, Al, and the fact is I really don't want to integrate with you. Nothing personal, but that's the way I feel."

"You refused to fuse with me?" Crompton asked, incredulous.

"That's it," Loomis said. "I'm really sorry, I know you've come a long way for nothing; though you might have written first and asked me, you know? Anyhow, my apologies, but that's how it is."

"Are you unaware," Crompton said, "that you are incomplete, unfinished, a caricature of a man rather than a complete portrait? Don't you know that your only possibility of dragging yourself out of the gutter of your life into the clear, godlike atmosphere of self-transcendence is through fusion with me?"

"I know," Loomis said with a sigh. "And sometimes I do have the desire to find something pure, sacred, serene, and untouched by the hands of men."

"Well then?"

"But frankly, I don't think about that sort of thing too much. I can get by without it, you know? Especially now that Gilliam has split and I can start getting around a little more. I'm just having too much fun to give it all up in order to take up residence in your head, Al, no insult intended."

"Your present state of happiness is only temporary, as you must be aware. It will soon pass, like all of the other ephemeral things in your life, and you will return to the misery that has haunted most of your existence."

"Actually, it hasn't been so bad," Loomis said. "I really don't mind going right on with it just the way it's been."

"Then consider this," Crompton said. "Your personality resides in a Durier body, which has an estimated competence of forty-five years. You are thirty-five now. You have no more than ten more years to go."

"Hmmm," Loomis said.

"That means that in ten years, you'll be dead."

"I understand what it means," Loomis said. Thoughtfully he lighted a handmade cigarette with a red dot near the filter.

"Reintegration won't be so bad," Crompton said, twisting his face into agreeable lines. "We'll all do our best, you and the other fellow we still have to get in touch with. We will settle our differences in a rational, amicable manner and it will all be fine. What do you say?"

Loomis thought hard, drawing on his cigarette. At last he sighed and said, "No."

"But your very life—"

"I simply can't get worked up about that sort of thing," Loomis said. "It's enough for me to dig each crazy moment as it trundles past. Ten years is a long time, something's bound to turn up."

"Nothing will turn up," Crompton said. "In ten years you'll be dead. Just dead."

"Well, you can never tell. . . ."

"Dead!"

Loomis said, "Must you keep on saying that?"

"It's true. You *will* be dead!"

"Yeah, it *is* true," Loomis said. He thought and smoked. Then his expression brightened. He said, "I guess we'll just have to do this fusion, then."

"Now you're talking!"

"In about nine years."

"That's quite impossible," Crompton said. "Do you think I am simply going to hang around this ridiculous planet for nine years waiting for you to make up your mind?"

"Well—what else can you do?" Loomis asked reasonably. "Come on, old man, let's not quarrel. I have always found that things have a miraculous way of working themselves out if you simply ignore them and go about your business. Come with me, Alistair. I want to ask your opinion on something."

He led Crompton downstairs to a basement workshop. In one corner there was something that looked a little like an electronic organ. It had many switches and buttons and foot pedals, and resembled the cockpit of an anachronistic 747. There was a little footstool in front of it. Loomis sat down and turned on the power.

"This," he said to Crompton, "is a Wurlitzer-Venco Self-Expression Machine."

He flicked switches with both hands. "Now I have energized it and set the tone-values. The predominant mood, as you can tell from the clear yellows and oranges projected on the wall in front of you, is one of deep self-pity. This I further embellish through the musical theme which the machine will now produce, and also through the verses which it will write and reproduce in the lower left-hand corner of the big screen to your left. Listen, Alistair."

Loomis emoted at the machine, and the machine translated his emotions into colors, forms, rhythms, into chanted verse, into dance forms danced by elegant puppets, into gray ocean and black night, and into bleeding purple-edged sunsets suffused with sunburnt laughter and shaken by tremors of impotent rage. Misty, multicolored scenes came into focus, filled with odd wispy people who enacted dramas of curious import; and in these various representaglia, as they were technically called, one could feel the childhood dreams of the man, his first bewildering sexual cravings, his long and agonized school days, his first love on his second summer holiday, and much, much more, all flowing to the present, woven and intertwined in all of the art forms available in this series (except for soapbubble sculpture, a brand-new feature available only with the new Mark V Wurlitzer-Venco) and coming at last to the brilliant and paradoxical coda in which all the various elements were subordinated to their proper place in the ensemble of qualities that made up the projected image of the man, yet each highlighting and evoking the individuality of the others, and thus bringing out—by default, as it were—its own uniqueness. And so it ended and the two men were silent for a time.

At last Loomis said, "What do you think? Be completely frank; politeness is misplaced at a time like this."

"Well then," Crompton said, "I must tell you that is exactly what everyone plays on Self-Expression Machines."

"I see," Loomis said frigidly, pinching his nose in a gesture of inner pain.

He sat for a time, brooding silently. Then presently he cheered up and said, "Well, what the hell! It's only a hobby! I just dabble at it, you know. But I do think I achieved some pretty effects for an amateur, don't you? Let's get together for a drink sometime. How long did you say you were staying?"

"Only long enough to Reintegrate you," Crompton said.

"Then it's going to be a long stay," Loomis said. "Because I'm staying just the way I am."

He turned back to the Self-Expression Machine and played a cheerful little piece compounded of the sounds, smells, and images of lust, greed, and intoxication. Crompton left before the reprise.

13

He wandered aimlessly through the streets, uncertain of his next move. His glittering premise had broken apart. Somehow it had never occurred to him that Loomis, a mere segment of himself, and not too bright a segment at that, might prefer to go it through life alone.

He pulled himself together sufficiently to hail a taxi. It was a six-legged semiliving Ford Vivacoupe—the XFK model with the 240-cubic-inch stomach and the hemispheric kidneys. He fitted his feet into the stirrups, gave the address of his hotel to the built-in driver surrogate, and lolled disconsolately against the well-worn pommel. By divergent paths the bitter insight came to him: better love's disreputable counterfeit than the eternal highwire act on the slippery catenaries of your own nerves. He was very close to tears at that moment.

The taxi clattered down the incident-strewn streets of Cetesphe. Crompton, preoccupied with his misery, did not even notice the Testercian funeral procession that passed, led by the corpse itself, gaily decked in harlequin colors, his flippers animated by minute electrical impulses directed by the priest-technicians nearby.

The Hotel Granspruinge came into sight, but Crompton indicated to the taxi that it should drive on. A certain unstable dynamism—the product, perhaps, of helplessness times insecurity—had invaded his being. Though normally a well-controlled man, even by his own stringent standards, he had decided that this was the time for the occasional crazy plunge he did allow himself.

"Do you happen to know," he asked the taxi, "where I could find a Moodalizer Den?"

The taxi, though only half alive, and not gifted with intelligence in the usual sense of that word, was nevertheless able to make an immediate U-turn and proceed down a narrow alley until it came to a store which bore a flashing neon sign reading: JOE'S MOODALIZER.

Crompton got out of the taxi and paid. He entered the Moodalizer, trembling slightly from anticipation. What he was doing wasn't really *wrong*, he had to remind himself.

The proprietor, a bald sweating fat man in an undershirt, looked up from his comic book long enough to indicate an empty cubicle to Crompton. Crompton went in and quickly stripped down to his underwear. His breath came more heavily as he fitted the electrodes into place on his forehead, arms, legs, and chest.

"All right," he called out, "I'm ready to order."

"Okay," the fat man said. "You know the rules. You get one from Column A and one from Column B. Our selections for the day are printed on the menu on the wall."

Alistair scanned the selections. "Under Column A— State of Mind—I think I'd like number five, Courageous Equanimity. Unless you'd recommend sixteen, Daring Insouciance?"

"It's running a little thin tonight," the fat man said. "If I were you I'd stick with five. Or try seventeen, Satanic Cunning, very piquant tonight with especially selected Oriental emotional ingredients. I can also recommend twenty-three, All-wise Compassion."

"I'll stick with five," Crompton said. "Now for Column B, Contents of Mind. I think I'd like a nice number twelve, Tight-packed Logical Thought Forms Garnished with Mystic Insights and Sprinkled with a Seasoning of Understanding and Humor."

"That's always a good one," the fat man said. "But let me suggest our special tonight, number one thirty-one, Inspirational Associations under Pale Rose Jelly Visions, and Garnished with Humor and Pathos. And we are famous for our number seventy-eight, Whole Sensuality Thoughts Served on a Bed of Butterfly Random Insights with a Topping of Humor and Gravity."

"Could you possibly let me have two from Column B? I'd make it worth your while."

"Can't do it, buddy," the fat man said. "Too great a risk for you. It could send you into terminal oscillation, and lose me my license."

"Then I'll take twelve from Column B, but leave out the humor." (These places sprinkled it over everything.)

"Right," the fat man said. He set his instruments. "Get ready. Here it comes!"

Crompton felt the familiar sense of wonder and gratitude as the current hit. He was suddenly calm, utterly serene, and filled with a joyous sense of certainty. Energy and stability flooded through him, and with them came insights of great subtlety and depth. Crompton saw the vast and complex cobwebbing that connects all parts of the universe, and he was at the center of it, in his rightful place in the Scheme of Things. Then he understood that not only was he a man, he was also all men, and an axiomatic expression of the commonality of the species. Inviolable joy welled up in him; he possessed the will of Alexander, the wisdom of Socrates, the scope of Aristotle. He knew what things were all about. . . .

"Time's up, buddy," the fat man called out as the machinery clicked off.

Crompton tried to hold on to the splendid mood which the Moodalizer had induced, but it slid away from him and he was himself once more, and trapped in the claustrophobic confines of his situation. All he was left with was a fragile and indistinct memory. But that, though intangible, was still something.

He returned to his hotel room feeling marginally better.

Soon he grew despondent again. He lay on his bed and felt sorry for himself. It really was unfair! He had come to Aaia with the perfectly reasonable expectation of finding in Loomis a creature even more miserable than himself, a thin and inadequate personality disgusted with the futile inanities of his existence and eager, no, pathetically grateful for a chance to attain wholeness.

Instead he had found a man well pleased with himself, a man content to continue wallowing in the brutish sensual pleasures that all authorities agree can never bring true happiness.

Loomis did not want him! This inexplicable and astounding fact undermined the very basis of Crompton's planning and left him without apparent recourse. For you cannot coerce a part of you into joining the rest of you. This is a law of nature as old as exfoliation.

But he had to have Loomis.

He considered his options. He could leave Aaia and go to Ygga, find and incorporate the other aspect of his personality, Dan Stack, then return and try again with Loomis. But the two planets lay half a galaxy apart, the logistics were too tricky and the costs too great, and it was a lousy idea anyhow. Loomis had to be dealt with immediately, not put off until another time.

But perhaps he should give up the whole mad venture. Why not go to some pleasant Earth-type planet, and there make whatever adjustments he could on his own? It wouldn't be so bad. There was, after all, a certain joy in hard, dedicated work, a sort of pleasure in denying oneself pleasures, and a sour happiness to be found in steadiness, circumspection, dependability . . .

To hell with that!

He sat up on the bed, his narrow face set in lines of determination. So Loomis refused to fuse with him? That was what Loomis thought! Little did Loomis know of Crompton's iron will, his tenacity, his unshakable resolve. Loomis was selfish, stubborn only when the mood was on him, perseverant only when things were going his way. And he was subject to the rapidly changing moods that are the hallmark of the unstable cyclothymic pleasure-seeking personality.

"Before I'm through with him," Crompton said, "he'll come crawling to me on his hands and knees, begging to be taken in."

It would call for patience; but that was Crompton's chief asset. Patience, cunning, determination, and a measure of ruthlessness—those were the qualities by which Crompton expected to capture his butterfly-minded component.

Master of himself once again, Crompton mentally reviewed his circumstances. He realized at once that he could not remain in the Hotel Grandspruinge. It was much too

expensive. He needed to conserve his money against unknown contingencies.

He packed, settled his bill, and went out and hailed a
taxi. "I need a cheap room," he told the driver. "Sí
hombre, por qué no?" the driver responded, and proceeded
across the Bridge of Sighs that connects luxurious downtown Cetesphe with the slums of East Cetesphe.

14

The taxi took Crompton deep into the notorious Pigfat district of South Cetesphe. Here the streets were narrow and
cobblestoned, and ran, or rather, staggered, through numerous compound windings and adventitious turns. A per-
manent yellowish gray fog lay over the district, and the
gutters were uniformly full of slops. Although it had been
midday when Crompton left the Grandspruinge, in Pigfat it
was always dusk going on night.

The driver took him to a sagging five-room tenement
building. The sign outside of it read: ROOMS, CHAMBRE,
ZIMMER, GWEGWELFEISSE, ULMUCH'THUN. It was obviously an interstellar rooming house of the lowest class.

Within, seated at a three-legged cardtable that passed
as a reception desk, sat an old, humpbacked crone with a
cast in one eye and a raven on her shoulder.

"A room, is it?" she asked. "Lord, yes, you're in luck,
we just do happen to have a vacancy since they took poor
Mr. Crank out of 12-B this morning, or rather shoveled
him out, him being in an advanced state of putrescence,
poor lamb."

"What did he die of?" Crompton asked.

"Tertiary envy, that's what the intern said. Here is your key. Your room is on the top floor underneath the eaves, and you've got a nice view of the fishmeal factory."

Crompton unpacked, then went out for a look at his new district.

Pigfat was certainly a most strange and incongruous sight after the rational wonders of Cetesphe proper. Pigfat was dark, dangerous, dank, and malodorous, and had been carefully planned that way by the Aaians some years ago when they had decided to import slum crime in order to see if there was anything amusing or significant in it. The programmatic origin of the squalor made it no less disgusting in Crompton's eyes.

He walked down innumberable wretched streets, past over-flowing garbage cans and smoldering mattresses. Yellow-eyed cats watched him with an air of savage calculation. A thin sulfurous ground-mist clung to his legs, and a gritty wind tugged at his coattails. From boarded-up tenement windows came the sounds of children crying, couples coupling, dogs howling.

From a nearby saloon he heard coarse shouts of mirth and drunken merriment. Crompton walked quickly past. Suddenly the batwing doors burst open and a man came through and hurried up to Crompton, seizing him familiarly by the arm.

"Where are you going in such a hurry, Professor?" the man asked in a friendly voice.

Crompton favored him with a look that could have withered skunk cabbage at ten paces. "Sir, I do not believe we are acquainted."

"Not acquainted!" the man said. "Mean to say you don't remember good old Harry Stygmatazian who did a six-month stretch with you at Luna Penitentiary for aggravated bunco?"

Harry Stygmatazian was a small, fat, balding man with wet spaniel eyes and a pug nose.

"My name is not Professor," Crompton told him. "I have never been to Luna. And I have never seen you before."

"That's beautiful," Stygmatazian said, falling into step beside Crompton. "You're such a con artist, Professor, I'd actually think you didn't know me if I didn't know better."

"I don't know you!"

"Don't worry, we'll play it your way," Stygmatazian said. "We'll pretend we just met."

Crompton walked, and Stygmatazian hurried along beside him. "I guess you just got in, huh, Professor? A lot of the boys are here already. It's quite an opportunity, isn't it?"

"What are you talking about?" Crompton asked.

"The Aaian special offer. All next month they are going to let us plunder their homes in the best parts of town, insult their women, beat up tourists, and generally crud the place up, and with no interference from anyone. They say that they want to experience moral outrage. But you know all about this."

"The Aaians have actually invited you here to rob them?" Crompton asked.

"They've even laid on special charter flights for criminals who qualify. You gotta hand it to the Aaians, they really get into the spirit of things."

"It is incomprehensible to me," Crompton said.

"But profitable, huh, Professor?"

"Stop calling me Professor!"

Stygmatazian shook his head admiringly. "You're one in a million, Professor, you never crack. Six months we shared a cell in Luna, and you never once during that time let on that you so much as knew my name. And here you are still keeping it up! That's what I call control."

"Leave me alone!" Crompton shrieked, and turned back the way he had come. Behind him he could hear Stygmatazian explaining to a disinterested bystander, "That's the Professor. He and I did a stretch together in Luna. You could learn a few things from a man like that."

15

Stygmatazian must have spread his story far and wide, because Crompton found that there was considerable respectful curiosity about him throughout the Pigfat district. For the first time in his life, strangers came up and asked whether they could buy him a drink. Women made clear their sudden interest in him by rubbing themselves slowly up and down against his barstool. Crompton enjoyed all of this, but he also detested it, since he knew that it was not him they were interested in but some imaginary construct in their dull and doubtless diseased minds.

Then one morning, Nature, which abhors static situations, threw in a catalyst to get things moving again. The catalyst came in the form of a very large, powerfully built, brutally handsome young man with blond hair and blue eyes who sat down opposite Crompton one morning while he was eating his customary oatmeal and melba toast.

"Hope you don't mind the intrusion, Professor," the big man said in a genial voice. "I heard you was in town and I am a longtime admirer of your coups and triumphs in the confidence racket. Is it true that you was the mastermind behind the plot to infiltrate the FBI with degenerate Albanian communist faggot lepers?"

"It is a lie. Kindly go away and leave me alone," Crompton said.

"Now that ain't no way to talk to an admirer," the big man said. "It's lucky for you that you are a hero of mine, because otherwise I would probably mash your head in. My name is Billy Berserker. Hurting people is my business,

73

but I'm trying to get into a better-paying field. That's where you come in."

Crompton opened his mouth to expostulate, then thought better of it as he observed the dancing red sparks in Berserker's blue eyes.

"What do you want of me?" he asked.

"Let's go to a place I know," Berserker said. "I'll tell you all about it."

Later, in a sequestered booth in the back of the Al Capone Memorial Tavern in East Pigfat, Billy Berserker told about himself. Berserker was a pseudonym he had adopted, a *nom de crime*. His real name was Edwin Gastenheimer, and he had been brought up in Paterson, New Jersey, the son of Charles G. Gastenheimer, an internationally famous bank robber, and Elvira Gastenheimer, who operated the infamous Giggles Club in Hoboken. Young Edwin had sought to emulate his successful and upwardly-mobile parents. He served the usual apprenticeship in the stews of Jersey City, then went to Columbia University, where he was proclaimed Psychopathic Personality of the Year three times running. He was a natural as a smash-and-grab man or an enforcer; but the higher reaches of crime were outside his abilities. And so it went, the dull years of living and hurting people, the hopelessness of it all. There seemed to be nothing he could do to better himself. And then he heard of the new opportunities to be found on Aaia.

"And that's where you come in, Professor," Berserker said. "Fate has thrown us together like this. I need your help to change my life. I am now going to reveal my deepest ambition to you, the secret pulsating soul of a man. So please do not laugh at me or I might kill you in a characteristic moment of sudden unreasoning rage that has more than earned for me my sobriquet, Berserker."

"What is it that you want?" Crompton asked.

Berserker looked momentarily shy. In a low voice he said, "Professor, more than anything else in the world I want to be a confidence man and live by my wits."

Crompton thought about that. "And you believe that I can help you?"

"I know you can! You will be my guru, and I will

follow your advice and example. Men *can* rise on stepping-stones of their dead selves to higher things!"

In his excitement Berserker pounded the table for emphasis, driving a spoon two inches deep into the hardened formica surface. The gesture was not lost on Crompton, who considered the hopeful, murderous, and probably insane man in front of him and decided that there was nothing to do but get into the situation and hope for the best.

He took a deep breath and heard himself say, "My boy, there is no reason why you should not make a first-rate confidence man. You have a confident bearing already. That is very important in this sort of thing, as I am sure you can appreciate. Your speech is straightforward, and no man would think you had much guile. In brief, your air of bucolic ferocity is an excellent mask beneath which, we both know, hides a rapierlike incisiveness of intellect. Yes, my boy, there will be no trouble at all."

"Gee, that's great, Professor," the giant said. "You're talking just the way I thought you'd talk."

"How gratifying," Crompton said.

"But now, what should I do specifically?"

"Ah, yes," Crompton said, thinking desperately, "we do come down to the practicalities of the situation. We must find something for you to do. To do. . . . Well, you must learn! You must learn all the little tricks of dress and address that go to make up the truly accomplished confidence man."

"That's just what I need!" Berserker said. "You see, I don't really know how a confidence man acts, and I don't want to look ridiculous by thinking I'm looking like one when I'm not. That would embarrass me, and when I'm embarrassed I get angry."

"Obviously you must study," Crompton said. "And how? By observing the movements and manners of a top confidence man who happens to be here on the planet Aaia."

"You mean you!"

"No, not me. My con is drabness. That would never do for you. You need to copy a confidence man with flair, good appearance, daring—the very qualities that you yourself possess, though in vestigial form."

"Gosh, Professor, is there really such a man upon this planet?"

"There is, and you must observe him. That means standing fairly near him and watching what he does at all times. You must keep on watching until you have learned all of his mannerisms. Thus can you master the style and address of a master confidence man."

"Who is this guy?" Berserker demanded.

"His name is Edgar Loomis," Crompton said. "I will write down his address for you."

16

From Loomis's Journal:

Yesterday I attended the Cridrru Ball, one of the main events of the year. Everybody of any note in Cetesphe was there, including Elihu Rutinsky and several movie stars whose names I didn't quite catch. I wanted to be seen there, of course, since it pays one to be seen, no matter what your line of work. But I had another motive as well. Miss Cissy Perturbsky was going to be there.

The ball was held in the Axiomatic Room of the Hotel Geometry. I drove up in a cerise Gondolini I had borrowed for the occasion, wearing a body stocking made up entirely of silverfoil ruffles.

But let me skip ahead to the good part— Cissy and I, alone together in one of the little bedrooms that adjoin the main ballroom. We had just slipped in on impulse; and now, beneath a single dim spotlight, Cissy was smiling, peering at me with her pretty, lustful little cat's face. We had met briefly last year at a party. Something had definitely passed between us at the time, but we had been taken up with other people and it had been inconvenient to follow up on what was, after all, an unspoken acknowledgement of a future possibility.

But here she was at last, slim-hipped and pert-breasted, just as I remembered her, and with that uptilt to the eyes that gave her so exotic an aspect and raised in me fantasies of slave and master games. Her lips were parted. She moistened them and said, "So . . . You have not forgotten me?" Her faint Hungarian accent drove me near distraction. I mastered myself and said coolly, "Sure, baby, how you been keeping?" (A touch of callousness, of brutal indifference, it's the only way to play the game.)

Her eyes widened. Like a sleepwalker she came to me, and her arms clasped themselves around my neck. Her breasts pressed into my silverfoil ruffles, flattening them as she stretched herself on tiptoe to reach my downturned, sneering lips. It was really a marvelous moment. And then somebody in the darkened interior of the bedroom sneezed.

We broke apart. I turned on the lights and saw a large blond man sitting in a love seat in one corner. He had a notebook in his hand and was scrawling in it with a pencil stub.

"There had better be some good explanation for this," I gritted ominously.

The blond man stood up. I saw that he was very large indeed.

"Just keep right on doing whatever you're doing, bub," he said. "I'm studying you."

"Are you, indeed?" I asked. "Why?"

"Because I want to be like you."

Cissy had exited at this point. Better luck next time! I conversed with Billy Berserker, as he was called, and learned that someone called the Pro-

fessor had sent him to study me. A few words of
description were enough. That damnable Crompton!

"Of course you can study me," I told Berserker, when it became obvious that I had no
choice in the matter. "As a matter of fact, I've
been looking around for a disciple, someone to
pass on my precious store of knowledge to."

"How lucky that we met!"

"Isn't it, though? I will contact you soon and
tell you what our course of study is to be. Just
write your address and phone number on this
piece of paper. Then go home and prepare yourself for really hard and challenging work."

He shook his head: he wasn't buying it. "I'll
choose the times myself, and I'm beginning right
now."

"I'm the teacher," I pointed out. "I know
what's best."

"Yeah, but I don't trust you yet."

"So what do you propose to do?"

"I'm going to hang around you all the time
and watch you, like the Professor said I should."

"My dear fellow! That would be quite impossible. For one thing, I would be unable to act
in a characteristic manner—the uncertainty principle in human relations, if you see what I mean.
And so there would be nothing for you to study."

Berserker jutted his jaw at me in an unpleasant manner and said, "Either you'll act in a characteristic manner or I'll beat the hell out of you."

"What good would that do? No confidence
man is able to act with confidence after he's been
beaten up."

He stopped to consider that. I could almost
feel the sluggish relays in his brain opening and
closing, bringing him simplified message-units
that he could barely comprehend. At last he said,
"If you don't act confidently like a confidence
man, then I'll kill you and find someone else to
copy."

I forced out a jolly little chuckle. "But I'm
the best," I reminded him. "In fact, I'm the only

first-rate confidence man on this planet. You'd have to go copy some second-rater, which would make you third-rate at best."

"I really want to learn from you," he said. "I see that you got a lot of class."

"Now you're talking," I said, giving him a playful punch on the arm. "We'll do it my way and you'll be a confidence man in no time."

"Thank you," he said. "But as my first act of confidence I am going to do it my way by sticking to you and observing you all the time like the Professor said I should."

And that was his last word on the subject. A tough one indeed for yours truly! But never fear, I shall figure something out.

17

From Gilliam's Secret Diary:

Well, I've finally done it—walked out on Ed, even though he obviously didn't want me to go. What a relief it was at first! But then Gwend-kwifer started acting up, and there was nothing happening, and I started to think how nice it used to be with Ed every once in a while, so I told him I'd changed my mind, I wanted to come back, and the bastard told me to get lost!

I know it's all the influence of that bird-faced little pal of his. Ever since he's come, Ed has been just a wild man. (Ed's always been a bit wild anyhow, of course. He tells me that's because of his Sicilian ancestry on his mother's side. I'm just a fool for these third-world types.)

And Gwendkwifer is really bugging me. She keeps on saying that she misses Daddy, and that's all right, but when she says she misses Daddy's *girlfriends*, that's really too much, and from my own daughter, too. I really don't understand why I have to take this crap. Did I go to Radcliffe in order to hear that kind of jazz?

Well, at least I've finally made up my mind to take Ed back in spite of that he deserves nothing better than a stake through his heart for the rotten werewolf bastard that he is. But he *is* Gwen's father, and he's not much worse than any other man. But the problem is that Ed doesn't realize that he wants me back. It's all the fault of that runty little twerp who claims to be some sort of relative of Ed's. I couldn't get the story straight, I guess it's complicated in these Sicilian clans. Maybe he's cast a spell over Ed, or maybe Ed is trying to prove some stupid male thing. He's always been sorta flippy, but this time he's getting too far out.

New entry:

I've been making a few phone calls and keeping my eyes open and I see that Ed is hanging around all the time with this big blond guy I never saw before. *Where does he fit in?* Those two are thicker than thieves and it all seems very pally and perverted and sick. Could Ed be having a homo thing? I wouldn't put it past him just to spite me. But I think something else is going on.

New entry:

That big blond guy also knows Crompton! So the three of them are up to something! But what could it be? I think I better find out what's going on.

18

Crompton was quietly doing a crossword when there was a loud knock at the door. He opened it and Gilliam stormed in, demanding to know what he was trying to do to her husband.

"I want him to join me," Crompton said calmly.

"What do you mean, join you? It sounds like some kind of a circus act."

"Don't you know the situation?" Crompton asked. "The virus schizophrenia, the Durier bodies, Reintegration?"

"I saw a special on it once on the TV. Do you mean to say that you and Ed—"

"We are some of the results of a case of virus schizophrenia," Crompton said. "We are two parts of the same personality. There's another of us, also, Dan Stack, who lives on the planet Ygga. We are three separate parts of a single personality. None of us can be complete without the others."

"Go on," Gilliam said.

"Do you understand about the Reintegration process? The other two parts of my personality—Loomis and Stack—have the opportunity now of giving up their bodies (which are only Duriers anyhow) and joining me in my own, human body. After that—with a little luck—comes the actual process of fusion and transformation in which we become a new and competent personality."

"Not so fast," Gilliam said. "I'm still thinking about

81

the body thing. Everybody joins you, huh? That's cozy. And I suppose you stay in charge?"

"Well," Crompton said, "I *am* the most competent personality, and it *is* my body."

"And what happens to *their* bodies?"

"They just collapse and die. But it's not actual death, because the personality, the intelligence, the I that knows itself as Edgar Loomis, will survive."

"Well, I see it all now," Gilliam said. "And the answer is no."

"I beg your pardon?"

"He is not going to get away with it."

"What are you talking about?"

"This little number that you and Ed have cooked up together." She laughed scornfully. "Does he actually think he's going to walk out on me by letting his body die while his so-called personality goes traipsing off to distant planets? Not a chance, brother, not a chance. I'm sure there's some law that says he can't legally become someone else while he's still legally my husband. Otherwise what is the marriage vow worth? Any court in the galaxy would back me up on that one."

Before Crompton could answer—if he had any answer—she had walked out and slammed the door behind her.

19

Several days later, Crompton and Loomis met for lunch at
Casa Orthodontia, the only Mexican restaurant on the
planet Aaia. Crompton arrived late, and was shown to his
table by the proprietor, stately plump Al Dente.

"About time you got here," Loomis said. He was well
dressed, as usual, today with a terrycloth jumpsuit styled
by Tony of Pimlico. His shoes, with tinkly chimes built into
the heels, were by Harbinger & Omen. Despite his elegance, however, Loomis did not look well: a faint tremor
of the lower lip betrayed his inner perturbation.

After studying the menu, Crompton ordered the con-
servative Combination Plate Two. Loomis went for super-
exotic Thirty-seven. They exchanged banalities for a while.
Then Loomis could stand it no longer.

"Look here, Crompton," he said, "you've really got to
stop it."

Crompton raised an eyebrow in interrogation.

"You know very well what I'm talking about. I refer
to that gigantic blond oaf you sicked on me."

"You refer to Billy Berserker?"

"He's changing his name to Sammy Slick," Loomis
said. "He's living with my wife now, it may interest you to
know. That's the only good development in this whole
mess. The only way I get any time to myself is when he's
with her, which isn't very often, damnably enough. He
sticks to me closer than my shadow—he's even around in
the dark!"

"He's a serious-minded young man," Crompton said.

"But he'll never make a con guy. He ought to take up haunting people, that's what he's really good at."

"Why don't you suggest it to him?"

"He'd just write it down in his notebook and keep on following me. Crompton, you have to get him off my back! I can't function with him around! Seducing rich women just doesn't work when he's around! Alistair, whatever your grievance with me, it is unfair to take away a man's livelihood."

Crompton bit down firmly on an enchilada made entirely of carrots and walnuts, then wiped his lips with a precise gesture. "Loomis," he said, "your plea is not pertinent to the context. This is not a disagreement between two individuals. It is a quarrel between parts of the same personality. The circumstances are unusual, I grant you, but that is the heart of the situation. There are no rules to cover internalized conflicts."

"But I don't see it that way," Loomis said. "You're leaving a few things out. True, we are parts of the same personality; but I'm also a separate and distinct being, and the law recognizes my status as such. I have the inalienable right to not Reintegrate with you if I don't want to."

"I've thought about this a great deal," Crompton said. "I know that you have the legal right to do as you please; but not the moral right. Or, to put it differently, I have the moral obligation to bring us back together again."

"I don't see why," Loomis said.

"In my opinion," Crompton said, "I'm merely following an evolutionary law: an organism must fight to renew itself, or accept degeneration and death. The law of life—if you'll excuse the expression—tells me to repair my damage. There's no real question of like or dislike. If it were a matter of my own personal taste, I'd be inclined to forget this whole thing and try to live content with what I happen to be. But life has given me the opportunity to heal myself, and I must pursue it whether or not you—or I, for that matter—like it."

They ate for several minutes in silence. Crompton found the manchas mantecas not to his liking, but enjoyed the refried beans topped with pumpkin-seed sauce. Big Al Dente, with his starchy grin and quick businessman's pop-eyes, came by to enquire if everything was satisfactory, then left to serve Billy Berserker, who had just sat down at an adjoining table with his notebook and pencil stub.

Loomis concentrated for a moment on spearing a bit of seviche. When he looked up his eyes were cold.

"Now listen to me carefully, Alistair," he said slowly, with careful emphasis. "I am essentially an easygoing, easy-living, easy-forgiving sort of fellow. It is alien for me to carry a grudge, and downright unlikely for me to contemplate violence. But I am willing to make an exception in your case. You are pressing me too damned far."

"Go play it on your Self-Expression Machine," Crompton said, with that quick thrust of cruelty to which he was growing accustomed.

The roots of Loomis's nostrils became pinched and white. He rose with dignity. "Very well, Alistair. You think that you are the only one with willpower and determination? We shall see. Just remember that I warned you."

He walked out of the restaurant followed by Berserker, who winked at Crompton.

20

That evening, as Crompton was about to leave for a walk, his door was suddenly flung open. Loomis stepped in, looked quickly around, shut the door behind him and locked it.

"All right, we'll do it your way," he said. "I've decided to Reintegrate with you."

Crompton's initial feeling of joy was stifled in a wave of suspicion.

"What made you change your mind?"

"Does it really matter? Can't we just get on with it?"

"First I want to know why," Crompton said.

"It's a little difficult to explain. Can't we save that for later, after we—"

There was a heavy pounding at the door. Berserker's deep voice shouted, "I know you're in there, Loomis! Come out, or I'm coming in after you."

Loomis's hands were trembling uncontrollably. "I have a dread of physical violence. And anyhow, he's a lot bigger than I am. Alistair! Please!"

"Tell me," Crompton said implacably.

Beads of sweat appeared on Loomis's forehead. "Gilliam came to see me today, and one thing led to another. You know how it is."

"I know how it is with you," Crompton said. "So what happened?"

"That crazy Berserker found us in bed together and went crazy with jealousy? Can you believe it? Someone trying to kill me because I slept with my own wife? I could laugh if it weren't so terribly terrible what that madman is going to do to me."

The door began to splinter under repeated blows. Crompton turned to his personality component.

"Come," he said, "let's Reintegrate."

The two men stared into each other's eyes, parts calling for the whole, potential increasing to bridge the gap, new gestalten trembling on the verge of being. Then Loomis gasped and his Durier body collapsed, folding in on itself like a rag doll. At the same moment, Crompton's knees buckled as though a weight had fallen on his shoulders.

The hinges gave way. Billy Berserker marched into the room.

"Where is he?" Berserker shouted.

Crompton pointed to Loomis's body on the floor.

"Oh," said Berserker, momentarily nonplussed. "Well, he was a lousy bastard and he really deserved it. But who am I going to learn from now? Professor, what should I do?"

"Go back to hurting people," Crompton said. "It's what you're really good at."

THREE

21

The journey from Aaia to Ygga was a long one, whether measured in light-years or in units of subjective experience. The new navigational equipment was not yet installed on this run, so the ship—the Western Galactic Clipper—had to travel in the slow, old-fashioned way, via adventitious helices in the pseudospace structure.

Crompton did not object to the leisurely pace. It allowed him a badly needed rest from the discontinuities of Aaia, and afforded a chance to get to know the person with whom he was sharing his head.

Reintegration had not taken place, of course, since it is possible only when all the constituent elements of a personality have been brought together, and even then is not inevitable.

Loomis was extremely silent and withdrawn on the first day. Crompton was barely aware that he was there. But after a good night's sleep, Loomis seemed considerably recovered. He accepted Crompton's invitation to a game of shuffleboard, each man taking turns at controlling the body. They were very polite to each other, and deferential to each other's wishes, like strangers forced by circumstance to share a room for the night.

The honeymoon ended on the afternoon of the third day. Crompton had lunched lightly, taken a nap, then a cold shower, and was working on a crossword puzzle.

After a while, Loomis said, "I'm bored."

Crompton said, "Why don't you help me with this puzzle? It's really enormous fun once you get into it."

"No, no," Loomis said, and his emotion of distaste was so strong that it made Crompton wince.

"What would you like to do, then?"

Loomis brightened immediately. "What say we go to the ship's bar and check out some action for ourselves?"

"Action?"

"Women. Or woman. I forgot, we'll only need one."

Crompton sat bolt upright. In a tight voice he said, "We will not require any women."

"We won't?"

"Absolutely not."

"What's the matter, you gay or something? Because if you are, we'll just have to work something out."

"My sexual interests are perfectly normal," Crompton snapped. "But I do not intend to do anything about them at present."

"Why not?" Loomis asked mildly.

"I have my own reasons."

"I see," Loomis said calmly. "Well, it's entirely up to you, of course."

"I'm glad you're being so reasonable."

"To each his own, as the philosopher said. No skin off my teeth. Why don't you take a nap for a few hours while I borrow the body and do my thing?"

"Oh, no," Crompton said. "That is most definitely out of the question."

"Hey, wait a minute," Loomis said. "Don't *I* have any say in what this body does?"

"Of course you do," Crompton said. "In other areas you will find me more accommodating. I suggest that you turn to one of your other interests or hobbies for the present."

"Sex is my only hobby," Loomis said, "as well as being my business. Be reasonable, Al! You can't just make believe it's not there. Sex is a normal, physical need, you know, like eating."

"I am well aware of that," Crompton said. "But I happen to believe that the act of intercourse with a beloved person goes beyond the merely physical, that it is indeed a holy thing, the epitome of caring, and therefore must be—ah—*performed* only in circumstances of beauty and tranquillity."

"Alistair," Loomis asked, "are you by any chance a virgin?"

"What has that to do with it?" Crompton demanded furiously.

"I thought so," Loomis said sadly. "I believe we should have a little talk about sex. It is indeed a splendid and spiritual thing, just as you have always pictured it. But you left something out."

"What?"

"The fact that sex is also fun. You have heard about fun, haven't you?"

"I've always wanted to have some," Crompton said wistfully.

"Then don't give it another thought. Just let me take over for a while. Fun happens to be my best area. Did you check out that little blonde at lunch? Or maybe you'd prefer to shop around a little more first?"

"What you are intimating is completely out of the question!" Crompton cried.

"But Al! My health and mental stability require—"

"My decision is final," Crompton said. "It *is* my body, you know. I will try to make this up to you in other ways. But the subject of sex is closed."

Loomis made no further comment, and Crompton thought that the delicate subject had been disposed of. Several hours later he was disabused of this notion when they sat down to dinner in the ship's main restaurant.

"Don't eat the shrimp," Loomis said as the appetizer was served.

"Why not? You like shrimp. We both like shrimp."

"It doesn't matter. We're not eating it."

"Why not?"

"Because it's *trayf.*"

"Beg pardon?"

"*Trayf* is a Jewish word that means that it is unclean food and is unfit for a Jewish person."

"But Edgar, you aren't Jewish."

"I have just converted."

"You've what? What are you talking about?"

"I have just become a Jew. An Orthodox Jew, as a matter of fact—none of your slipshod modern shortcuts for me, thank you very much."

"Edgar, this is ridiculous! It's impossible! You can't simply become a Jew just like that!"

"Why not? You think I'm incapable of having a religious revelation?"

"I've never heard anything so insane in my life," Crompton said. "Damn you! Why are you doing this?"

"To give you trouble, or *tsuris*, as we say in the ancestral language of my new religion. Frankly, I don't think we can eat any of this food."

"Why not?"

"It's obviously not kosher. I think we'd better speak to the steward. They must make some arrangement for people of my persuasion."

Crompton said, "We are not going to speak to anyone about this insane and blasphemous notion of yours! The whole thing is simply too absurd."

"Sure it's absurd, for a *goy* like you. Listen, do you think they've got a *shul* aboard this bucket? If I'm going to keep the dietary laws, I might as well pray, too. It couldn't hurt, right? And I want to ask the captain have we got any other *landslent* aboard, maybe we could get up a *minyan*, or at least a game of bridge."

"We're not going to speak to anyone! I refuse to go along with this!"

"You're prohibiting me from practicing my faith?"

"I am not going to let you make a fool of me and a mockery of religion!"

"So suddenly you're the big judge of religious feeling?" Loomis said. "I know what you are, Crompton—you're nothing but a redneck Cossack! *Oy*, it would be just my *mazel* to get stuck in the head of a bigot! Would it offend your sensibilities if I got a Bible from the ship's library and read it quietly to myself? I'll do it in the cabin so it won't embarrass you."

"Loomis, please! You're making me very nervous. People are starting to look at me." (Loomis and Crompton's conversation was silent, of course, but something of its dialogic nature was inevitably displayed by the facial muscles, especially those around the eyes. When the talk really got going, Crompton looked like a *ticquer* on speed.) "Couldn't we eat our dinner quietly and then discuss— ah—the entire situation?"

"Do you mean the *entire* situation?"

"That's what I said."

"Crompton, are you trying to bribe me away from my newly found religion?"

"Certainly not. I just think we can work out some sort of adult solution to . . . everything. Come on, have some soup."

"Well, what kind is it?"

"Chicken barley. Just have a taste."

"Maybe a *bissel*. But if you think that means—"

"Later, we'll talk," Crompton said. "Now eat your soup, *please*."

The dinner proceeded quietly, though Loomis did insist upon humming "My Yiddische Mama" between courses. After they had finished, without discussion, Crompton lapsed into a passive, dreamy, blurry state in which he absentmindedly relinquished control of the body.

With deft casualness Loomis took over and made conversation with the giggly red-haired woman at the next table. She turned out to be the wife of a lockwheel configurator from Druille V, taking a brief holiday to see her parents on Ygga. Her name was Alice-June Neti. She was small, bright-eyed and vivacious. She had a slender though sumptuous figure. She was bored by the long journey through space.

Detached, floating free from it all, Crompton watched with muzzy interest as intimacy progressed through winks and nods and gestures and little suggestive comments not always in the best of taste. Soon they were dancing, and then Loomis generously receded, leaving Crompton in command of the body's volition—nervous, flushed, tanglefooted, and enormously pleased with himself. And it was *Crompton* who led her back to the table, *Crompton* who made small talk with her, and *Crompton* who touched her hand, while the complacent and Machiavellian Loomis looked on.

At 3:00 A.M., ship's time, the ship's bar closed. After a final exchange of pleasantries with Alice-June, Crompton reeled back to his cabin on B deck and collapsed happily on the bed. This evening had been the most fun he had ever had in his whole life. He wanted to lie on the bed now and savor it. But this was not Loomis's idea at all.

"Well?" Loomis asked.

"Well what?"

"Let's have a quick piss and get going. The invitation was clear enough."

"I didn't hear any invitation," Crompton said, puzzled.

"She told you her room number rather pointedly," Loomis said. "That, together with the events of the evening, constitutes more a demand than an invitation."

"Is that really how this sort of thing works?" Crompton asked.

"It's one of the more typical ways."

"I just can't believe it!"

"Take my word for it, Alistair, I do have some slight degree of expertise in these matters. Let's get going."

Crompton struggled to his feet, then collapsed across the bed again. "No, I wouldn't . . . I couldn't . . . I mean to say, I haven't . . ."

"Lack of experience is no problem whatsoever," Loomis said, firmly pulling them to a sitting position. "Nature is exceedingly generous in helping one to discover how to do what She considers important for creatures to do together. I will bring to your attention the fact that beavers, racoons, rattlesnakes, scarab beetles, and other creatures without a hundredth of your intelligence manage to perform what you find so baffling. You mustn't let down the species, Al!"

Crompton got to his feet, wiped his glowing forehead, and took two tentative steps toward the door. Then he walked back and sat down once again on the bed.

"I'm afraid it's out of the question," he said.

"But why?"

"It would be unethical. The young lady is married."

"Marriage," Loomis said patiently, "is a human invention of very recent origin, considering the history of *homo sapiens*. But before marriage there were men and women, and certain sexual modes between them. Natural law always takes precedence over human legislation."

"I still think it's immoral," Crompton said, without much vigor.

"But how could you possibly think that?" Loomis asked, astonished. "You are unmarried, so no possible blame can attach to *you* for your actions."

"But the young lady is married."

"Of course she is. That's her responsibility, not yours.

She is first and foremost a human being, not some mere chattel of her husband. She has the God-given right to make her own decisions, and I believe that we must respect that."

"I never thought of it that way," Crompton said.

"So that takes care of her. Finally, there is the husband. He will know nothing of this, and therefore will not be injured by it. In fact, he will gain. For Alice-June, in recompense, will be much nicer to him than she's been in some time. He will assume that this is because of his forceful personality, and his ego will be beneficially bolstered thereby. So you see, Al, it's one of those situations that comes along every once in a while in which everyone gains and nobody loses. Isn't that nice for us?"

"It's all a lot of sophistry," Crompton grumbled, standing up again and walking toward the door.

"Right on, baby," said Loomis.

Crompton grinned idiotically and opened the door. Then a thought struck him with invincible compunction and he slammed the door shut and lay down again on the bed.

"What's the matter now?" Loomis asked.

"Those reasons you gave me," Crompton said, "may or may not be sound. I don't have enough experience of this sort of thing to know. But there is one thing I do know. *I will not engage in anything of this sort while you are watching!*"

Loomis was taken aback. "But damn it, Al, there is no you or me. I'm you! You're me! We're two parts of the same personality!"

"Not yet we aren't," Crompton said. "At present we exist as separate schizoid parts, two different people in a single body. Later, after we've taken in Dan Stack and the three of us go into true Reintegration . . . Well, it will be different then. But under the present circumstances, my sense of decency forbids me from doing what you suggest. It is simply unthinkable and I do not wish to discuss it any further."

Loomis lapsed into furious silence. Crompton undressed, put on his pajamas, and went to bed.

22

"It seems to me," Crompton said the following morning over coffee, "that you and I must have a serious discussion."

"What's on your mind, buddy?" Loomis asked with offensive cheerfulness.

"I wish to remind you that we are engaged in an important and dangerous enterprise. We must find and incorporate Dan Stack, and do it quickly, for our own situation is delicate and precarious in the extreme. We have no time for drunkenness and fun; all that will be possible in due time. But for now there is work to be done. There must be no repetition of last night. Do I make myself clear?"

Loomis's thoughtform expressed a civilized and rueful weariness. "Alistair, you really are difficult to get along with. I know it's all terribly serious, but right now we're sitting in a spaceship without anything to do."

"I have thought about that," Crompton said. "We can employ our time most usefully at present by learning haut-Yggal, the main language of the planet we are going to."

"Learn a *language*, just like that? I have no aptitude for that sort of thing."

"Then you can watch quietly while I learn."

In the ship's library, Crompton found a copy of Bender's *Dialectical Variations of Various Common Expressions in Haut-Yggal*. He began to study. Loomis amused himself by rerunning his memories of the previous night until Crompton asked him to desist, as it interfered with his concentration.

96

After lunch, Crompton took a nap, then exercised for an hour, then worked on a crossword puzzle. Loomis made no objections. But in the early evening he did request a glass of beer. Crompton was glad to comply with this request. He was not entirely prudish.

The beer tasted just a little strange. Crompton commented on this to Loomis. Loomis said something, but Crompton lost the words in the vast and shuddering emptiness that had just opened around him. Tables, chairs, dust motes, and bright yellow napkins had begun a stately procession around him as he passed out.

The next thing Crompton knew it was morning. Puffy-eyed, flatulent, and with an unbelievable headache, he dragged himself out of bed. His cabin looked as if Tamerlane and a regiment of the Golden Horde had held a victory celebration there last night. The floor was littered with bottles, and the ashtrays were filled with skinny little butts. Various garments were still strewn around, and some of them were unmistakably feminine. Cheap perfume filled his nostrils, and it was mingled with the acrid chemical odor of illegal stupefacients.

Crompton tottered to his feet. He felt pain in his left thigh. Looking down, he saw tooth-marks. He also noticed a smear of feminine cosmetics on his chest.

There were other signata of sexual incontinence too embarrassing for Crompton even to acknowledge.

"Loomis," he said, "you drugged me and perpetrated a nauseating debauch using my body last night. What do you have to say for yourself?"

"Only that I am through taking orders from you," Loomis declared spunkily. "What gives you the right to tell me what to do or not do? I'm not your slave! I am legally your equal! Hereafter, *you* may run the body by day and study whatever you please; but *I* shall have it to myself in the nights!"

Crompton forced himself to remain calm. "You will have control of this body only when and for how long I allow you."

"But that's not fair!"

"I would be glad to give you an equal share in operating the body if you were willing to shoulder even a minimal share of the responsibility. But since you do not care for useful behavior, I must act in terms of the better interests of both of us."

"What makes you the big judge of useful behavior? It's typical fascist-pig thinking."

"Watch your mouth," Crompton warned.

"Fuck you, fascist pig!"

At that, Crompton's thin edge of control crumpled. Red rage consumed him, and he was swept by the imperious desire to destroy his detestable alter ego. Caught off guard by this flood of destructive emotion, Loomis tried to rally, to fight back, to maintain his psychic equilibrium.

His struggle was to no avail. Crompton's rage produced a sudden massive flood of antidols—units of psychic energy whose function is to expugn pain. Loomis fought back furiously: he knew that if the antidol process went to completion, he could be lost forever, walled off, encysted in a forgotten cul-de-sac in Crompton's mind.

"Alistair!" he screamed. "Don't do it! You need me to Reintegrate with!"

Crompton heard him and knew what he said was true. He fought down the unexpected blood-lust still singing in his veins and grasped at his remaining modicum of sanity. With a main heave he imposed control over his raging emotions.

The antidol cordon swiftly collapsed, leaving Loomis shaken but unhurt.

For a while they weren't on speaking terms. Loomis sulked and brooded for an entire day and swore that he would never forgive Crompton's brutality. But he had no talent for hating. Above all he was a sensualist, living the moment, forgetful of the past, incapable of worry about the future. His resentments soon passed, leaving him with his normal sunny disposition.

Crompton recognized his responsibilities as the dominant part of the personality. Regretting his murderous outburst, he worked hard at making himself agreeable. For the rest of the flight they maintained a good, though careful, relationship.

At last they reached Ygga. They were sent down to the Induction Satellite, where they passed through customs and immigration. They received injections to prevent Creeping Fever, Green River Plague, Elbow Rot, Knight's Disease, Chorpster's Syndrome, and Halloran's Itch. They were then permitted to take the shuttle down to Yggaville.

23

Ygga was the sole planet of the gray dwarf star Ioannis (BGT 344590). A pear-shaped world with an oscillation moment of seven degrees seven minutes at apehelion, Ygga had a terranormic rating of .65892, and a typical Class C spread of minerals except for the sole and unaccountable absence of molybdenum.

The planet had four continents, three of which were buried under lava and were accordingly uninhabited except by microscopic lava-eaters and their parasites. The fourth continent, Clorapsemia, had a landmass roughly equivalent to Asia and Africa combined. Meandering in an undulent and deckle-edged ribbon along Ygga's equator, this continent recapitulated a climate and flora and fauna roughly equivalent to some of the better years of Earth's Carboniferous Age.

The autochthonous, indigenous, and eponymous race of Ygga, the Yggans, were of remote reptilian ancestry. Standing about eight feet tall, extremely strong and agile, bloodthirsty and of a crude sense of humor, the Yggans were a menace to the Terran minority that controlled their planet. An undeclared war smoldered between the two races, complicated by the fact that the Yggans could not be legally killed, being protected by interstellar protocols. Terrans were not protected from the Yggans by a similar law, however, since the Yggans did not recognize any law except their own, which no one else recognized. Their unruly ways were condoned only because it was usually just worthless, jobless Terrans who got killed, whereas otherwise they would be eligible for social benefits. In addition, this arrangement tended to obscure the knowledge that the Yggans were a dying race whose birthrate had fallen to zero ever since the Terrans had sprayed their planet with Supercyclone B, a gas that induces sterility in reptiles and in certain rare types of moths.

Yggaville, the chief city of northwest Clorapsemia continent, was a tropical sort of place with broad dusty boulevards decked out in open-air stalls where grinning natives sold handchewn tata-bark refulgences for the flourishing art deco market on nearby Nesbitt IV.

At City Hall, Crompton subverted a stubborn clerk into releasing Dan Stack's last known address. This was in the city of Inyoyo, a musk-pearl collection point on the left bank of the Greenish River. To reach this place was no easy task, however, for Inyoyo lay behind the Great Swamp of Kilbi, which covered an area equal to all of Western Europe excluding Albania. To cross this one had to join an expedition, and Crompton found one that was departed the following morning.

After a restless night at the Hotel Ygga, where swarthy plantation owners held noisy reunions with shrill blond harpies until dawn, Crompton went to Collection Street, the starting point for the expedition.

Trips into the interior were organized with considerable care. The most important feature of every expedition, of course, was its falaya craft. These were boats with hulls made of a local balsa-wood-type plant, ovoid in shape and capable of bearing the weight of a dozen men, or of two ziernies.

The ziernies were the bell-hoofed hornless oxen of Ygga, the standard transport across the swamplands. The ziernies were physically similar to the East Indian water buffalo, differing mainly in having sphincter muscles around their fore-kneecaps, for a reason no one had ascertained. These great, tireless beasts were capable of plodding rapidly through the soupy mixture of sand, water, clay, malt, and borax crystals that made up the greater part of the swamp. When aroused, the ziernies were capable of attaining speeds of five miles an hour, or better, slapping the water with their bell-shaped feet and creating a partial vacuum through which the falaya craft could easily be towed. The drawback of the ziernie was its tendency to metamorphose unexpectedly into its alternate form, which was long and flat and batlike and of no use to Terrans whatsoever. In this way they differed considerably from their Terran cognates, but were good-tempered and sweet-smelling brutes despite that.

At considerable expense Crompton rented his own ziernie, driver, and falaya craft. He also had to purchase a knapsack, folding tent, pink plastic washbasin, canteen with orange canvas cover, two compasses, a supply Compactoplex food pellets, a Swiss Army knife, and a miniature collator with twelve-month charge.

At last everything was ready. The wagonmaster gave two warning blasts on the traditional rhinoceros-hide bugle, then one more. The expedition set off, accompanied by the deep-throated singing of the Yggan paddlers. Their chant can be roughly translated as follows:

By diverse and paradoxical means the spirit of mud
Consigns grief to the heavens and sharp wings to the face
That haunts the watery wastes of the dark swamp Mother
Whose trace is her ritual and whose somber sweet nostrils.

The exact meaning of this plaintive and evocative text awaits the publication of a definitive book on Yggan psychology. For now, it can only be pointed out that, in common with many tribal chants throughout the galaxy, obscurity is made to carry a heavy burden.

24

Loomis claimed at first that he wanted to participate in the operation of the body. But this was not exactly true. What Loomis wanted was to be there for the interesting parts. He wanted to taste the varied flavors and textures of food, experience the sensation of thirst-quenching, look at fascinating objects and hear amusing sounds. But he didn't want to be in conscious control and full sensory contact during the nasty spells.

The interminable days of traveling through the swamp seemed to be made up mostly of nasty spells. "Take over," Crompton would say, and abruptly Loomis would be tipped out of the dreamy mental domain that he usually inhabited into the seat of consciousness. One moment he would be floating along in a disembodied high, drifting on the waves of images that dimly limned the external world for him, blurrily, as through a translucent screen; the next instant, pow! he's in the head, looking out of the eyes—those gritty, tired eyes—sick of staring at the monotonous gray-green vegetation or the grimy, insect-bitten backs of the bearers.

But the visual impact was the least of it. Consider the olfactory situation: plunged from his odorless cocoon into the dusky pungencies of the bearers, the burnt-meat smell of rotting vegetation, the unbearable chlorine-and-violet odor of the ziernie's stools, all combined with the sharp ammoniac scent of Crompton's own perspiration.

How Crompton himself—possessor of one of the human race's truly discriminating noses—could stand this cacophonous stench, and do so uncomplainingly, was a measure of the hard-driving stoicism of the man. Loomis considered the situation to be frankly unbearable. (The odors of alien places are difficult to describe, but frequently subsume the essence of a place more vividly than the more usual visual description. Who will forget Clarenden's statement that Alkmene V smells "exactly like a bison's fart delivered through a vat of rancid goat's cheese"? Or Grignek's statement about Gnushi II—"an aroma rather like the amalgamation of molasses and cold cream in the belly of a putrefying anteater"?)

But even smell was not the worst of it. What was really intolerable was that Loomis, all sleepy and good-natured and lazy, had to take over and feel the maddening itching of Crompton's eczema, had to caw angrily through aching throat at the skylarking bearers, had to feel the continual anxiety of waiting for a possible native attack, and worst of all, had to make continuous effort to push the tired body onward, resisting the desire to call a halt, take a break, give up he whole damned thing.

Loomis, who had never wanted to begin this insane journey toward a goal whose attainment he could only judge as highly dubious, was also supposed to take over Crompton's motivation when he took over Crompton's body, and that was really asking too much. Here was this idiot, jeopardizing both their lives against Loomis's strongest protests, and Loomis was supposed to aid and abet him? He would not! Loomis resisted in accordance with one of the deepest instincts of human beings: the urge not to be a complete shmuck.

Therefore, Loomis's character is not to be impugned by first reluctance and then his outright refusal to aid Crompton in crossing the vast swamp. Loomis, at this point, was not an ally. He was a captive, allowed a measure of light and freedom only so long as he cooperated with his jailer. It is to his credit that he continued to fight for identity and for life itself with the feeble weapons at his disposal.

He was, after all, a person in his own right, though admittedly in unusual circumstances. And despite what has been said about the behavioral rigidity and inadequacy of a single isolated personality segment, Loomis really got on very well in the world. A lot of people with so-called whole personalities would be doing damned well if they could get a tenth of the fun that Loomis had.

Loomis knew that Crompton thought of him as a mere means to an end, a thing to be used to transform Crompton into Super-Crompton through the ingestion and assimilation of his mind-brothers. It was not a very pleasant thought. Loomis had to live with it, but he really hoped he wouldn't have to go along with it.

25

"Want to pop for ten?" the ziernie driver asked Loomis.

"Why not?" Loomis replied. He had been sent by Crompton to exercise the body while Crompton caught a few hours of well-deserved sleep. Loomis had been acting tolerably well recently, except for his incessant bellyaching and his misguided attempts to undermine the fighting spirit that was the only thing that sustained Crompton with his unsubtle assertions that "every single one of us is going to be killed on this crazy fiasco trip." He was not one of your silent sufferers.

Now Loomis was engaged in a game of Ouuve with the ziernie driver. This particular ziernie driver was a grook, as the Yggan-born creole population of Ygga was called. He had wagered heavily on the outcome of the next throw, and his normally smooth face grew lumpy with anxiety as he watched Loomis hold the twin crystals by their scribed side, breathe a prayer on them, and then cast them into the teakwood scoring cone.

The crystals rattled; a lucky spin trapped them in the blue spiral gravure, scoring a top twenty for Loomis and leaving him victor.

The ziernie driver turned pale under the sparse yellow fuzz on his face. He had been relying on the well-known luck of the grooks, and it had turned bad on him, as usual. The grooks didn't have any luck because they were too stupid to realize that they just weren't lucky. Since the ziernie driver could not pay, that would mean extreme chastisement at the hands of Old Rukth, the strongest and most stupid of the expedition's grooks, whose ritual function was to enforce the grooks' hallowed concepts of racial inferiority.

"Listen, mister," the grook whined, "I've got something better for you than money. I've got secret information that a gentleman of your obvious intelligence would find of considerable interest and perhaps of practical value as well."

"Can't pay, huh?" said Loomis. He eyed the ziernie driver keenly. A small smile tugged at the corner of his mouth until he brushed it away and he saw it land on the corner of someone else's mouth. "Well, hell, it doesn't matter. What is this information?"

The grook leaned forward and whispered in Loomis's ear. Loomis's eyes widened. A frown crossed his face and he quickly brushed it off but allowed the smile to tug once again at the corner of his mouth.

"Interesting indeed," he said, "if true."

"Me no lie, effendi!" the grook squawked, in his panic relapsing absurdly into the patois of a people he could not even claim as his ancestors.

Crompton woke up abruptly. "What's going on?" he demanded.

Loomis gracefully relinquished control of the body. "Nothing much. I was just having a chat with this fellow here."

The ziernie driver cringed and scraped, then hurried away.

"Did you give our body a rubdown after its walk?" Crompton demanded.

"Of course! What do you take me for?"

"We won't go into that now," Crompton said. "How soon does the expedition get moving again?"

"Soon," Loomis said. "You know, Al, you're not looking so good."

Loomis was not referring to the objective facial appearance of the body they shared. He was speaking instead of the self-image which each of them projected to the other as his patent and indivisible individuality, and by means of which they communicated.

Crompton's self-image was visibly depleted, over-worked, strained. He had taken upon himself many of the chores which slow down expeditions. Aside from his own chores, he had planned out a perimeter defense against anhidis, the creeping dragon-grass that sometimes claims ten percent of an expedition. And he had organized the nightly distribution of the prized red points among the bearers, which formerly had been carried out in a haphazard manner with much cursing.

Loomis had remained faithful to his decision not to help. His own idea of how to find Dan Stack was to sign into a comfortable resort hotel somewhere and write Stack a letter. If that failed, they could always hire a detective agency.

Even Crompton lost track of how many days he had been in the swamp, hearing the incessant bat-shrill of the boo-hoo bird, the wet slapping grunt of the brown dotted crocopod, and the never-ending staccato of the compressed air extractors. They had beaten back two minor attacks by renegade and degenerate Ygga tribesmen disguised as patriots. Three children had been born to female members of the expedition, and scurvy was beginning to show up among the older unmarried males. The commissary had run out of tapioca pudding and was even forced to ration the oatmeal cookies.

Yet spirits were high, and the expedition moved onward, a complex microcosm traversing a wet spot.

At last, through a break in the lowering cloud cover, a high promontory was spied to westward. Soon you could make out the shale huts and white picket fences of Inyoyo.

The expedition had won through safely to its destination. All that remained was the question of who would get the first shower.

26

Inyoyo was a small place. Crompton made inquiries at the white clapboard post office just past the livery stable, and was directed at once to a weatherbeaten frame and shingle house on the edge of town. There, on a sagging veranda, he found two old people who acknowledged that they were Dan Stack's foster-parents.

"It's a fact," said the hard-bitten, deeply tanned old man with the prominent Adam's apple and the piercing faded blue eyes set in a bony high-cheekboned face. "I war the father, and she war the mother."

"And little Dan'l war a good boy," the old woman said.

"Well," said the old man.

"Well, it's true!"

"There war the incident of Mr. Wintermute's horse," the old man reminded her.

"They never proved that! You oughtn't to talk so sure less'en you hear the other side."

"But the horse can't talk now, Martha," the old man said.

"I didn't mean the *horse*, you simple-minded old greasebag! I meant that nobody's heard Dan'l's side."

"I reckon maybe that's cause he ran out of town like a thief in the night," the old man said, speaking with that exquisite precision that the uneducated sometimes attain after too much black coffee.

"Well, of course he run!" the old woman said indignantly. "He had to run, on account of they were trying to frame him with that bank robbery thing!"

"Do you happen to know where I could find him now?" Crompton asked.

"Couldn't rightly say," the old man said. "He never wrote us. But Billy Davis saw him Ou-Barkar that time he drove his semi there with a load of seed potatoes."

"When was that?"

"Five, maybe six years ago," the old lady said. "He could be anywhere now. Clorapsemia is a big continent, even if it is deckle-edged. You got a good face, mister! Go find him and straighten him out!"

She buried her face in her apron and cried. The old man accompanied Crompton past the old oak tree to the edge of the old plank road.

"You'll have to excuse my wife," he told Crompton. "Ever since Dan'l left, taking our tiny nest egg along with anything else of value he could lay his hands on, Ma just hasn't been the same."

"I understand," Crompton said. "I want you to know that I am going to find Daniel and make a whole man out of him."

"Piss on him," the old man said, spitting on his gnarled left fist in a gesture of uncertain ethnic origin, then turning and returning to his sagging veranda.

"This Stack guy really sounds like a fun person," Loomis commented. "Al, what are you getting us into?"

"He does sound a bit—unsavory," Crompton admitted. "But we really don't have any choice in the matter. Without him we can't Reintegrate."

Loomis sighed. "Where is this Ou-Barkar, anyhow?"

"It lies to the south," Crompton said, "in the deep unknown interior of this primeval planet."

"Oh, Christ! Not again!"

"I will get us there," Crompton said. "I have complete confidence in my ability to persevere despite straitened circumstances."

"I know, I know," Loomis said. "Wake me when it's all over." He went to sleep.

27

Ou-Barkar was a cluster of plantations where fifty Terrans supervised the work of two thousand aboriginals, who planted, tended, and harvested the li trees that grew only in that sector. The li fruit, gathered twice a year, was the basis of elispice, a condiment considered indispensable in Cantonese cooking.

Crompton met the foreman, a huge, red-faced man named Haaris, who wore a revolver on his hip and a blacksnake whip coiled neatly around his waist.

"Dan Stack?" the foreman said. "Sure, Stack worked here nearly a year. Then he left, sorta sudden-like."

"Do you mind telling me why?" Crompton asked.

"Don't mind at all," the foreman said. "But let's do it over a drink."

He led Crompton to Ou-Barkar's single saloon. There, over a glass of local corn whiskey, Haaris talked about Dan Stack.

"He came up here from East Marsh. I believe he'd had some trouble with a girl down there—kicked in her teeth or something. But that's no concern of mine. Most of us here aren't exactly gentle types, and I guess the cities are damned well rid of us. I put Stack to work overseeing fifty Yggans on a hundred-acre li field. He did damned well at first."

The foreman downed his drink. Crompton ordered another and paid for it.

"I told him," Haaris said, "that he'd have to drive his boys to get anything out of them. We use mostly Chipetzi tribesmen, and they're a sullen, treacherous bunch, though husky. Their chief rents us workers on a twenty-year contract, in exchange for guns. Then they try to pick us off with the guns. But that's another matter. We handle one thing at a time."

"A twenty-year contract?" Crompton asked. "Then the Yggans are practically slave laborers."

"Right," the foreman said decisively. "Some of the owners try to pretty it up, call it temporary indenture or feudal-transition economy. But it's slavery and why not call it that? It's the only way we'll ever civilize these people. Stack understood that. Big, hefty fellow he was, and handy with a whip. I thought he'd do all right."

"And?" Crompton prompted, ordering another drink for the foreman.

"At first he was fine," Haaris said. "Laid on with the blacksnake, got out his quota and then some. But he hadn't any sense of moderation. Started killing his boys, and replacements cost money. I told him to take it a little easier. He didn't. One day his Chipetzis ganged up on him and he had to gun down about eight before they backed off. I had a heart-to-heart talk with him. Told him the idea was to get *work* out, not to kill Yggans. We expect to lose a certain percentage, of course. But Stack was pushing it too far, and cutting down the profit."

The foreman sighed and lighted a cigarette. "Stack just liked using that whip too much. His Chipetzis ganged up again and he had to kill about a dozen of them. But he lost a hand in the fight. His whip hand. I think a Chipetzi chewed it off.

"I put him to work in the drying sheds but he got into another fight and killed four Chipetzis. That was too much. Those workers cost money, and we can't have some hothead idiot killing them off every time he gets sore. I gave Stack his pay and told him to get the hell out."

"Did he say where he was going?" Crompton asked.

"He said we didn't realize that the Yggans had to be wiped out to make room for Terrans. Said he was going to join the Vigilantes. They're a sort of roving army that keeps the unpacified tribes in check."

Crompton thanked the foreman and asked the location of the Vigilantes' headquarters.

"Right now they're encamped on the left bank of the Rainmaker River," Haaris said. "They're trying to make terms with the Seriid. You want to find Stack pretty bad, huh?"

"He's my brother," Crompton said, with a faint sinking sensation in his stomach.

The foreman looked at him steadily. "Well," he said after a while, "kin's kin. But your brother's about the worst example of a human being I've seen, and I've seen some. Better leave him alone."

"I have to find him," Crompton said.

Haaris shrugged fatalistically. "It's a long trek to Rainmaker River. I can sell you pack mules and provisions, and I'll rent you a native kid for a guide. You'll be going through pacified territory, so you should reach the Vigilantes all right. I *think* the territory's still pacified."

28

That night, Loomis urged Crompton to abandon the search. Stack was obviously a thief and murderer. What was the sense of taking him into the combination?

Crompton felt that the case wasn't as simple as that. For one thing, the stories about Stack might have been exaggerated.

But even if they were true, it simply meant that Stack was another stereotype, an inadequate and monolithic personality extended past all normal bounds, as were Crompton and Loomis. Within the combination, in fusion, Stack would be modified. He would supply the necessary measure of aggression, the toughness and survival fitness that both Crompton and Loomis lacked.

Loomis didn't think so, but agreed to suspend judgment until they actually met their missing component.

In the morning Crompton purchased equipment and mules at an exorbitant price, and the following day he set out at dawn, led by a Chipetzi youngster named Rekki.

Crompton followed the guide through virgin forest into the Thompson Mountains, up razorback ridges, across cloud-covered peaks into narrow granite passes where the wind screamed like the tormented dead; then down, into the dense and steamy jungles on the other side. Loomis, appalled by the hardships of the march, retreated into a corner of himself and emerged only in the evenings when the campfire was lit and the hammock slung. Crompton, with set jaw and bloodshot eyes, stumbled through the burning days, bearing the full sensory impact of the journey and wondering how long his strength would last.

On the eighteenth day they reached the banks of a shallow muddy stream. This, Rekki said, was the Rainmaker River. Two miles farther they found the Vigilante camp.

The Vigilante commander, Colonel Prentice, was a tall, spare, gray-eyed man who showed the marks of a recent wasting fever. He remembered Stack very well.

"Yes, he was with us for a while. I was uncertain about accepting him. His reputation, for one thing. And a onehanded man . . . But he'd trained his left hand to fire a gun better than most can do with their right, and he had a bronze fitting over his right stump. Made it himself, and it was grooved to hold a machete. No lack of guts, I'll tell you that. He was with us almost two years. Then I cashiered him."

"Why?" Crompton asked.

The commander sighed unhappily. "Contrary to popular belief, we Vigilantes are not a freebooting army of conquest. We are not here to decimate and destroy the natives. We *are* here to enforce treaties entered into in good faith by Yggans and settlers, to prevent raiding by Yggans and Terrans alike and, in general, to keep the peace. Stack had difficulty getting that through his thick skull."

Some expression must have passed across Crompton's face, for the commander nodded sympathetically.

"You know what he's like, eh? Then you can imagine what happened. I didn't want to lose him. He was a rough and able soldier, skilled in forest and mountain lore, perfectly at home in the jungle. The Border Patrol is thinly spread, and we need every man we can get. Stack was valuable. I told the sergeants to keep him in line and allow no brutalizing of the natives. For a while it worked. Stack was trying hard. His record was unimpeachable. Then came the Shadow Park incident, which I suppose you've heard about."

"I'm afraid I haven't," Crompton said.

"Really? I thought everyone on Ygga had. Well, the situation was this. Stack's patrol had rounded up nearly a hundred Yggans of an outlaw tribe that had been causing us some trouble. They were being conducted to the special reservation at Shadow Peak. On the march there was a little trouble, a scuffle. One of the Yggans had a knife, and he slashed Stack across the left wrist.

"I suppose losing one hand made him especially sensitive to the possible loss of the other. The wound was superficial, but Stack berserked. He killed the native with a riot gun, then turned in on the rest of them. A lieutenant had to bludgeon him into unconsciousness before he could be stopped. The damage to Terran-Yggan relations was immeasurable. I couldn't have a man like that in my outfit. He needs a psychiatrist. I cashiered him."

"Where is he now?" Crompton asked.

"Just what is your interest in the man?" the commander asked bluntly.

"We're related."

"I see. Well, I heard that Stack drifted to Port New Hazlen and worked for a while on the docks. He teamed up with a chap named Barton Finch. Both were jailed for drunk and disorderly conduct, got out and drifted back to the White Cloud frontier. Now he and Finch own a little trading store up near Blood Delta."

Crompton rubbed his forehead wearily and said, "How do I get there?"

"By canoe," the commander said. "You go down the Rainmaker River to where it forks. The left-hand stream is Blood River. It's navigable all the way to Blood Delta. But I would not advise the trip. For one thing, it's extremely

hazardous. For another, it would be useless. There's nothing you can do for Stack. He's a bred-in-the-bone killer.
He's better off alone in a frontier town where he can't do
much damage."

"I must go to him," Crompton said, his throat dry.

"There's no law against it," the commander said, with
the air of a man who has done his duty.

29

Crompton found that Blood Delta was man's farthest frontier on Ygga. It lay in the midst of hostile Grel and Tengtzi
tribesmen, with whom a precarious peace was maintained
and an incessant guerrilla war was ignored. There was
great wealth to be gained in the Delta country. The natives
brought in fist-sized diamonds and rubies, sacks of the rarest spices, and an occasional flute or carving from the
lost city of Altereine. They traded these things for guns and
ammunition, which they used enthusiastically on the trad-
ers and on each other. There was wealth to be found in the
Delta, and sudden death, and slow, painful, lingering death
as well. The Blood River, winding slowly into the heart of
the Delta country, had its own special hazards, which
usually took a fifty-percent toll of travelers upon it.

Crompton resolutely shut his mind to all common
sense. His component, Stack, lay just ahead of him. The
end was in sight, and Crompton was determined to reach
it. He bought a canoe and hired six native paddlers, purchased supplies, guns, ammunition, and arranged for a
dawn departure.

That night they were in a small tent which the commander had put aside for Crompton's use. By a smoking kerosene lamp Crompton was stuffing cartridges into a bandolier, his attention fixed on the immediate task, unwilling to look elsewhere.

Loomis said, "Now listen to me. I've recognized you as the dominant personality. I've made no attempt to take over the body. I've been in good spirits recently and I've kept you in good spirits while we tramped halfway around Ygga. Isn't that true?"

"Yes, it is," Crompton said, reluctantly putting down the bandolier.

"I've done the best I could, but this is too much. I want Reintegration, but not with a homicidal maniac. Don't talk to me about monolithic personalities. Stack's *homicidal*, and I want nothing to do with him."

"He's a part of us," Crompton said.

"So *what?* Listen to yourself, Alistair! You're supposed to be the part of us most in touch with reality. And you're completely obsessed, planning on sending us into sure death on that river."

"We'll get through all right," Crompton said, with no conviction.

"Will we?" Loomis asked. "Have you listened to the stories about Blood River? And even if we do make it, what will we find at the Delta? A homicidal maniac! He'll shatter us, Al!"

Crompton was unable to find an adequate answer. As their search progressed he had grown more and more horrified at Stack's unfolding personality, and more and more obsessed with the need to find the man. Loomis had never lived with the driving need for Reintegration; he had come in because of external problems, not internal needs. But Crompton had been compelled all his life by the passion for completion, transcendence. Without Stack, fusion was impossible. With him there was a chance, no matter how small.

"We're going on," Crompton said.

"Alistair, please! You and I get on all right. We can do fine without Stack. Let's go back to Aaia or Earth."

Crompton shook his head.

"You won't go back?" Loomis asked.

"No."

"Then I'm taking over!"

Loomis's personality surged in a surprise attack and seized partial control of the body's motor functions. Crompton was stunned for a moment. Then, as he felt control slipping away from him, he grimly closed with Loomis, and the battle was begun.

It was a silent war, fought by the light of a smoking kerosene lamp that grew gradually dimmer toward dawn. The battleground was the Crompton mind. The prize was the Crompton body, which lay shivering on a canvas cot, perspiration pouring from its forehead, eyes staring blankly at the light, a nerve in its forehead twitching steadily.

Crompton was the dominant personality; but he was weakened by conflict and guilt, and hampered by his own scruples. Loomis, weaker, but single-minded, certain of his own course, totally committed to the struggle, managed to hold the vital motor functions and block the flow of antidols.

For hours the two personalities were locked in combat, while the feverish Crompton body moaned and writhed on the cot. At last, in the gray hours of the morning, Loomis began to gain ground. Crompton gathered himself for a final effort, but he couldn't bring himself to make it. The Crompton body was already dangerously overheated by the fight; a little more, and neither personality would have a corpus to inhabit.

Loomis continued to press forward, seized vital synapses, and took over all motor functions.

By sunrise, Loomis had won a total victory.

30

Shakily Loomis got to his feet. He touched the stubble on his chin, rubbed his numbed fingertips, and looked around. It was *his* body now. For the first time since Aaia he was seeing and feeling directly and solely instead of having all sensory information filtered and relayed to him through the Crompton personality. It felt good to breathe the stagnant air, to feel cloth against his body, to be hungry, to be *alive!* He had emerged from a gray shadow-world into a land of brilliant colors. Wonderful! He wanted to keep it just like this.

Poor Crompton. . . .

"Don't worry, old man," Loomis said. "You know, I'm doing this for your own good also."

There was no answer from Crompton.

"We'll go back to Aaia," Loomis said. "Things will work out."

Crompton did not, or could not, answer. Loomis became mildly alarmed.

"Are you there Al? Are you all right?"

No answer.

Loomis frowned, then hurried outside to the commander's tent.

"I've changed my mind about finding Dan Stack," Loomis told the commander. "He really sounds too far gone."

"I think you've made a wise decision," the commander said.

"So I should like to return to Aaia immediately."

The commander nodded. "All spaceships leave from Yggaville, where you came in."

"How do I get there?"

"Well, that's a little difficult. I suppose I could loan you a native guide. You'll have to trek back across the Thompson Mountains to Ou-Barkar. I suggest you take the Desset Valley route this time, since the Kmikti Horde is migrating across the central rain forest, and you can never tell about those devils. You'll reach Ou-Barkar in the rainy season, so the ziernies won't be able to trek to Inyoyo. But you can join the salt caravan traveling through Knife Pass, if you catch up to them in time. If you don't, the trail is relatively easy to follow by compass, if you compensate for the variation zones. Once you've reached Depotsville the monsoon will be in full career. Quite a sight, too. Perhaps you can catch a heli to New St. Denis and another to Yggaville; but I doubt it because of the zicre. Winds like that can mess up aircraft rather badly. So perhaps you'd best take the paddleboat to East Marsh, then a freighter down the Inland Zee. I believe there are several good hurricane ports along the southern shore, in case the weather grows extreme. I personally prefer to travel by land or air. The final decision of route, of course, rests with you."

"Thank you," Loomis said.

"Let me know what you decide," the commander said.

Loomis thanked him and returned to his tent in a state of nerves. He thought about the trip back across mountains and swamps, through primitive settlements, past migrating hordes. He visualized the complications added by the rains and the zicre. Never had his freewheeling imagination performed any better than it did now, conjuring up the horrors of that trip back.

It had been hard getting here; it would be much harder returning. And this time, his sensitive and aesthetic soul would not be sheltered by the patient, long-suffering Crompton. *He* would have to bear the full sensory impact of wind, rain, hunger, thirst, exhaustion, and fear. *He* would have to eat the coarse foods and drink the foul water. And *he* would have to perform the complicated routines of the trail, which Crompton had painfully learned and which he had ignored.

The total responsibility would be his. He would have

to choose the route and make the critical decisions, for Crompton's life and for his own.

But could he? He was a man of the cities, a creature of society. His life problems had been the quirks and twists of people, not the moods and passions of nature. He had avoided the raw and lumpy world of sun and sky, living entirely in mankind's elaborate burrows and intricate ant-hills. Separated from the earth by sidewalks, doors, windows, and ceilings, he had come to doubt the strength of that gigantic grinding machine of nature about which the ancients wrote so engagingly, and which furnished such excellent conceits for poems and songs. Nature, it had seemed to Loomis, sunbathing on a placid summer day or drowsily listening to the whistle of wind against his window on a stormy night, was grossly overrated.

But now, shatteringly, he had to ride the wheels of the grindstone.

Loomis thought about it and suddenly pictured his own end. He saw the time when his energies would be exhausted, and he would be lying in some windswept pass or sitting with bowed head in the driving rain of the marshlands. He would try to go on, searching for the strength that is said to lie beyond exhaustion. And he would not find it. A sense of utter futility would pass over him, alone and lost in the immensity of all outdoors. At that point life would seem too much effort, too much strain. He, like many before him, would then admit defeat, give up, lie down, and wait for death. . . .

Loomis whispered, "Crompton?"

No answer.

"Crompton! Can you hear me? I'll put you back in command. Just get us out of this overgrown greenhouse. Get us back to Earth or Aaia! Crompton, I don't want to die!"

Still no answer.

"All right, Crompton," Loomis said in a husky whisper. "You win. Take over! Do anything you want. I surrender, it's all yours. Just please, *take over!*"

"Thank you," Crompton said icily, and took over control of the Crompton body.

In ten minutes he was back in the commander's tent, saying that he had changed his mind again. The commander nodded wearily, deciding that he would never understand people.

Soon Crompton was seated in the center of a large dugout canoe, with trade goods piled up around him. The paddlers set up a lusty chant and pushed onto the river. Crompton turned and watched until the Vigilantes' tents were lost around a bend in the river.

31

To Crompton that trip down the Blood River was like a passage to the beginning of time. The six natives dipped their paddles in silent unison, and the canoe glided like a water spider over the broad, slow-moving stream. Gigantic ferns hung over the river's bank, and quivered when the canoe came near, and stretched longingly toward them on long stalks. Then the paddlers would raise the warning shout and the canoe would be steered back to midstream, and the ferns would droop again in the midday heat. They came to places where the trees had interlaced overhead, forming a dark, leafy tunnel. Then Crompton and the paddlers would crouch under the canvas of the tents, letting the boat drift through on the current, hearing the soft splatter of corrosive sap dropping around them. They would emerge again to the glaring white sky, and the natives would man their paddles.

"Ominous," Loomis said nervously.

"Yes, quite ominous," Crompton agreed, growing over-awed by his surroundings.

The Blood River carried them deep into the interior of

the continent. At night, moored to a midstream boulder, they could hear the war-hums of hostile Yggans. One day, four canoes of Yggans pulled into the stream behind them. Crompton's men leaned into their paddles and the canoe sprinted forward. The hostiles clung doggedly to them, and Crompton took out his rifle and waited. But his paddlers, inspired by fear, increased their lead, and soon the raiders were lost behind a bend of the river.

They breathed more easily after that. But at a narrow bend they were greeted by a shower of arrows from both banks. One of the paddlers slumped across the gunwale, pierced four times. The rest leaned to their paddles, and soon were out of range.

They dropped the dead paddler overboard, and the hungry creatures of the river squabbled over his disposition. After that a great armored creature with crablike arms swam behind the canoe, his round head raised above the water, waiting doggedly for more food. Even rifle bullets wouldn't drive him away, and his presence gave Crompton nightmares.

The creature received another meal when two paddlers died of a grayish mold that crept up their paddles. The crablike creature accepted them and waited for more. He was a nuisance, but he protected his own: a raiding party of hostiles, seeing him, raised a great shout and fled back into the jungle. He clung behind them for the final hundred miles of the journey. And, when they came at last to a moss-covered wharf on the riverbank, he watched for a while, and then turned back upstream.

The paddlers pulled to the ruined dock. Crompton climbed onto it and saw a piece of wood daubed with red paint. Turning it over he saw written on it BLOOD DELTA. POPULATION 92.

Nothing but jungle lay beyond. They had reached Dan Stack's final retreat.

32

A narrow, overgrown path led from the wharf to a clearing in the jungle. Within the clearing was what looked like a ghost town. Not a person walked on its single dusty street, and no faces peered out of the low, unpainted buildings. The little town baked silently under the white noonday glare, and Crompton could hear no sound but the scuffle of his own footsteps in the dirt.

"I don't like this," Loomis said.

Crompton walked slowly down the street. He passed a row of storage sheds with their owner's names crudely printed across them. He passed an empty saloon, its door hanging by one hinge, its mosquito-netting windows ripped. He went past three deserted stores, and came to a fourth which had a sign reading STACK & FINCH. SUPPLIES.

Crompton entered. Trade goods were in neat piles on the floor, and more goods hung from the ceiling rafters. There was no one inside.

"Anyone here?" Crompton called. He got no answer, and went back to the street.

At the end of the town he came to a sturdy, barnlike building. Sitting on a stool in front of it was a tanned and moustached man of perhaps fifty. He had a revolver thrust into his belt. His stool was tilted back against the wall, and he appeared to be half asleep.

"Dan Stack?" Crompton asked.

"Inside," the man said.

Crompton walked to the door. The moustached man stirred, and the revolver was suddenly in his hand.

"Move back away from that door," he said.

"Why? What's wrong?"

"You mean you don't know?" the moustached man asked.

"No! Who are you?"

"I'm Ed Tyler, peace officer appointed by the citizens of Blood Delta and confirmed in office by the commander of the Vigilantes. Stack's in jail. This here place is the jail, for the time being."

"How long is he in for?"

"Just a couple of hours."

"Can I speak to him?"

"Nope."

"Can I speak to him when he gets out?"

"Sure," Tyler said, "but I doubt he'll answer you."

"Why?"

The peace officer grinned wryly. "Stack will be in jail only a couple hours on account of this afternoon we're taking him *out* of the jail and hanging him by the neck until he's dead. After we've performed that little chore you're welcome to all the talking you want with him. But like I said, I doubt he'll answer you."

Crompton was too tired to feel much shock. He asked, "What did Stack do?"

"Murder."

"A native?"

"Hell, no," Tyler said in disgust. "Who gives a damn about natives? Stack killed a *man* name of Barton Finch. His own partner. Finch isn't dead yet, but he's going fast. Old Doc says he won't last out the day, and that makes it murder. Stack was tried by a jury of his peers and found guilty of killing Barton Finch, as well as breaking Billy Redburn's leg, busting two of Eli Talbot's ribs, wrecking Moriarty's Saloon, and generally disturbing the peace. The judge—that's me—prescribed hanging by the neck as soon as possible. That means this afternoon, when the boys are back from working on the new dam."

"When did the trial take place?" Crompton asked.

"This morning."

"And the murder?"

"About three hours before the trial."

"Quick work," Crompton said.

"We don't waste no time here in Blood Delta," Tyler said proudly.

"I guess you don't," Crompton said. "You even hang a man before his victim's dead."

"I told you Finch is going fast," Tyler said, his eyes narrowing. "Watch yourself, stranger. Don't go around impugning the justice of Blood Delta, or you'll find yourself in plenty of trouble. We don't need no fancy lawyer's tricks to tell us right from wrong."

Loomis whispered urgently to Crompton, "Leave it alone, let's get out of here."

Crompton ignored him. He said to the sheriff, "Mr. Tyler, Dan Stack is my half brother."

"Bad luck for you," Tyler said.

"I'd really appreciate seeing him. Just for five minutes. Just to give him a last message from his mother."

"Not a chance," the sheriff said.

Crompton dug into his pocket and took out a grimy wad of bills. "Just two minutes."

"Well, maybe I could—damn!"

Following Tyler's gaze, Crompton saw a large group of men coming down the dusty street.

"Here come the boys," Tyler said. "Not a chance now, even if I wanted to. I guess you can watch the hanging, though."

Crompton moved back out of the way. There were at least fifty men in the group, and more coming. For the most part they were lean, leathery, hard-bitten no-nonsense types, and most of them carried sidearms and wore moustaches. They conferred briefly with the sheriff.

"Don't do anything stupid," Loomis warned.

"There's nothing I *can* do," Crompton said.

Sheriff Tyler opened the barn door. A group of men entered and came out dragging a man. Crompton was unable to see what he looked like, for the crowd closed around him.

He followed the crowd as they carried the man to the far edge of town, where a rope had been thrown across one limb of a sturdy tree.

"Up with him!" the crowd shouted.

"Boys!" came the muffled voice of Dan Stack. "Let me speak!"

"To hell with that," a man shouted. "Up with him!"

"My last words!" Stack shrieked.

The sheriff called out, "Let him say his piece, boys. It's a condemned man's right. Go ahead, Stack, but don't take too long about it."

They had put Stack on a wagon, the noose around his neck, the free end held by a dozen hands. At last Crompton was able to see him. He stared, fascinated by this long-sought-for segment of himself.

Dan Stack was a large, solidly built man. His thick, deeply lined features showed the marks of passion and hatred, fear and sudden violence, secret sorrow and secret vice. He had wide, flaring nostrils, a thick-lipped mouth set with strong teeth, and narrow, treacherous eyes. Coarse black hair hung over his inflamed forehead, and there was a dark stubble on his fiery cheeks. His face betrayed his stereotype—the Cholerie Humor of Air, caused by too much hot yellow bile, bringing a man quickly to anger and divorcing him from reason.

Stack was staring overhead at the glowing white sky. Slowly he lowered his head, and the bronze fixture on his right hand flashed red in the steady glare.

"Boys," Stack said, "I've done a lot of bad things in my time."

"You're telling *us?*" someone shouted.

"I've been a liar and a cheat," Stack shouted. "I've struck the girl I loved and struck her hard, wanting to hurt. I've stolen from my own dear parents. I've brought red murder to the unhappy natives of this planet, and to some humans besides. Boys, I've not lived a good life!"

The crowd laughed at his maudlin speech.

"But I want you to know," Stack bellowed, "I want you to know that I've struggled with my sinful nature and tried to conquer it. I've wrestled with the old devil in my soul, and fought him the best fight I knew how. I joined the Vigilantes and for two years I was as straight a man as you'll find. Then the madness came over me again, and I killed."

"You through now?" the sheriff asked.

"But I want you to know one thing," Stack shrieked, his eyeballs rolling in his red face. "I admit the bad things I've done, I admit them freely and fully. But boys, *I did not kill Barton Finch!*"

"All right," the sheriff said, "if you're through now

we'll get on with it."

"Finch was my friend, my only friend in the world! I was trying to help him, I shook him a little to bring him to his senses. And when he didn't come around, I guess I lost my head and busted up Moriarty's Saloon and fractured a couple of the boys. But before God I swear I didn't harm Finch!"

"Are you finished now?" the sheriff asked.

Stack opened his mouth, closed it again, and nodded.

"All right, boys!" the sheriff said. "Let's go!"

Men began to move the wagon upon which Stack was standing. And Stack, with a look of helpless desperation on his face, caught sight of Crompton.

And recognized him for who he was.

Loomis was speaking to Crompton very rapidly. "Watch out, take it easy, don't do anything, don't believe him, look at his record, remember his history, he'll ruin us, smash us to bits. He's dominant, he's powerful, he's homicidal, he's evil."

Crompton, in a fraction of a second, remembered Dr. Vlacjeck's estimate of his chances for a successful Reintegration.

Madness, or worse. . . .

"Totally depraved," Loomis was saying, "evil, worthless, completely hopeless!"

But Stack was part of him! Stack too longed for transcendence, had fought for self-mastery, had failed and fought again. Stack was *not* completely hopeless, no more than Loomis or he himself was completely hopeless.

But was Stack telling the truth? Or had that impassioned speech been a last-minute bid to the audience in hope of a reprieve?

He would have to assume Stack's good faith. He would have to give Stack a chance.

As the wagon was pushed clear, Stack's eyes were fastened upon Crompton's. Crompton made his decision to let Stack in.

The crowd roared as Stack's body plunged from the edge of the cart, contorted horribly for a moment, then hung lifeless from the taut rope. And Crompton reeled under the impact of Stack's mind entering his.

Then he fainted.

33

Crompton awoke to find himself lying on a cot in a small, dimly lighted room.

"You all right?" a voice asked. After a moment Crompton recognized Shieriff Tyler bending over him.

"Yes, fine now," Crompton said automatically.

"I guess a hanging's something of a shock to a civilized man like yourself. Think you'll be okay if I leave you alone?"

"Certainly," Crompton answered dully.

"Good. Got some work to do. I'll look in on you in a couple of hours."

Tyler left. Crompton tried to take stock of himself.

Integration . . . Fusion . . . Completion . . . Had he achieved it during the healing time of unconsciousness? Tentatively he searched his mind.

He found Loomis wailing disconsolately, terribly frightened, babbling about the Orange Desert, camping trips at All Diamond Mountain, the pleasures of women, luxury, sensation, beauty.

And Stack was there, solid and immovable, unmoved.

Crompton also knew that Stack was completely and absolutely *unable* to reform, to exercise consistent self-control, to practice moderation. Even now, in spite of his efforts, Stack was filled with a passionate desire for revenge. His mind rumbled furiously, a deep counterpoint to Loomis's shrill babbling. Great dreams of revenge swam in his head, gaudy plans to rip that damned Sheriff Tyler limb from limb, machine-gun the whole town, build up a body of dedicated men, a private army of worshippers of STACK, maintain it with iron discipline, cut down the Vigilantes, and set loose murder, *revenge*, fury, terror upon the world!

Struck from both sides, Crompton tried to maintain balance, to extend his control over the two personalities. He fought to fuse the components into a single entity, a stable whole. But the minds fought back, refusing to yield their autonomy. The lines of cleavage deepened, new and irreconcilable schisms appeared, and Crompton felt his own stability underminded and his sanity threatened.

Then Dan Stack, with his baffled reforming urge, had a moment of lucidity.

"I'm sorry," he said. "You need the other."

"What other?"

"I tried," Stack moaned. "I tried to reform! But there was too much conflict. So I schismed."

"You what?"

"Can't you hear me?" Stack asked. "Me, I was schizoid, too. Latent. It showed up here on Ygga. When I went to Yggaville, I got another Durier body, and fissioned."

"There's *another* of us?" Crompton cried. "Of course we can't Reintegrate without him! Who is it, where is he?"

"I tried," Stack moaned. "Oh, I tried! We were like brothers, him and me. I thought I could learn from him, he was so quiet and good and patient and calm! I *was* learning! Then he started to withdraw."

"Who was it?" Crompton asked.

"So I tried to help him, tried to shake him out of it. But he was fading away fast, he just didn't care any more, and I went a little crazy and broke up Moriarty's Saloon. But I didn't kill Barton Finch!"

"*Finch* is the last component?"

"Yes! You must go to Finch before he lets himself die, and you must bring him in. He's in the room in back of the store. You'll have to hurry. . . ."

Stack fell back into his dreams of red murder, and Loomis babbled about the blue Xanadu Caverns.

Crompton lifted the Crompton body from the cot and dragged it to the door. Down the street he could see Stack's store. *Reach the store*, he told himself, and staggered out into the street.

He walked a million miles. He crawled for a thousand years up mountains, across rivers, over deserts, through swamps, down caverns that led to the center of the Earth, and out again to immeasurable oceans, which he swam to their farthest shore. And at the long journey's end, he came to Stack's store.

In the back room, lying on a couch with a blanket pulled up to his chin, was Finch, the last hope for Reintegration. Looking at him, Crompton knew the final hopelessness of his search.

Finch lay very quietly, his eyes open, unfocused and unreachable, staring at nothing. His face was the broad, white, expressionless face of an idiot. Those placid Buddha features showed an inhuman calm, expecting nothing and wanting nothing. A thin stream of saliva ran from his lips, and his breathing was imperceptible. Least adequate of the three, he was the ultimate expression of the Earthly Humor of Phlegm, which makes a man passive and uncaring.

Crompton forced back madness and crawled to the bedside. He tried to force Finch to see him, recognize him, join him.

Finch saw nothing.

Crompton allowed the tired, overstrained Crompton body to slump by the idiot's bedside. Quietly he watched himself drift into irrationality.

Then Stack, with his despairing reformer's zeal, emerged from his dream of revenge. Together with Crompton he willed the idiot to look and see. And Loomis searched for and found the strength beyond exhaustion and fear, and joined them in the effort.

Three together, they came into mutual focus. And Finch, evoked by three-quarters of himself, parts calling irresistibly for the whole, made a final rally. A brief expression flickered in his eye. He *recognized*. And rejoined his suffering brothers.

FOUR

34

The city of Brenh'a is situated on an eastern arm of Ygga's Inland Zee, near the eastuary of the Blackheart River, the broad and sluggish stream which drains the interior marshlands of the Danaid Wilderness. Known as the Jewel of the Outback, Brenh'a is Ygga's newest major city, a quickly growing entrepot on the edge of the great unknown, serving the needs of the diverse peoples of Ygga and their friends. Brenh'a is civilization's first or last outpost, depending on which way you are going, and it gets a colorful crowd, especially on a Saturday night.

The most famous place in Brenh'a is undoubtedly Max's Caravanaserai Restaurant on Little Dug Street just behind the statue of John Chivvie, Sweet Singer of the Badlands. Max's is an institution—a sprawling collection of dining rooms serving the diverse cuisines of two dozen worlds. Here, and only here on all Ygga, the fastidious Neccharese of Rumble's Planet can get their bowls of scrambled brains and tubers; the far-traveling Drumfittie salesmen can sit down to their plates of decomposed cats in aspic; and the New Yorkers of Sol III can dine on their native cuisine of pastrami, souvlaki, and dill pickles.

Into this place one evening there came a short, scrawny Earthling. From the vermilion stains on his bush jacket one could tell that he had just come in from the Blood River country. He had a severe, clerkish, unsmiling face, and tightly compressed lips. He was in no way remarkable; but he did have a certain air of uneasy equilibrium and potential madness that boded no good.

The headwaiter registered all of this with his infallible sixth sense for impending impropriety, and immediately assigned Hertha Sims to wait upon him.

Hertha was a large, buxom, shapely woman with a large, buxom, shapely face framed in crisp good-humored orange curls. She was adept at cooling out weirdos. She was something of a weirdo herself.

"Something to start with?" she asked cheerfully, handing Crompton the large souvenir menu with its 3,003 items. "A drink, a snort, a fix? Whatever turns you on, we got it."

"Nothing to start with," Crompton said firmly. He studied the menu until he found the section called Terran Tidbits. "I will have Dover sole without butter, green salad with no dressing, and a large glass of milk. Also one piece of dry toast, and—"

He stopped in midsentence. Hertha waited, her pencil poised. She saw the customer's face go through a series of amazing contortions. Some struggle seemed to be taking place within him; his face was changing uncannily.

Hertha said sympathetically, "I know how it is when you just can't decide."

The customer composed himself with a visible effort. "You must excuse me," Crompton said, "we are having some difficulty in making up our minds—my mind, I mean."

"Take your time," Hertha said. "You're just in from the wilderness? Not much choice of what to eat out there."

"That's true," Crompton said. "This is the first time this particular problem has come up like this." His face began to twitch, its planes and angles changed, took on momentary expressions, changed again. Hertha thought it looked just like a couple of guys having an argument.

"All right," the customer said. "We will have the one-pound New York steak, rare, without vegetable."

"It's really good," Hertha said.

"And we will also have the Szechuan banquet. *And* the sole. I suppose this must seem very peculiar to you."

"If you could hear my life story," Hertha said, "you would know why nothing strikes me peculiar anymore. What would you like to drink with that?"

The customer's face contorted once again, then cleared. "We—I—will have a stein of Lucky Lager, a glass of milk, and a good French wine."

When the feast was served, Hertha noticed that the customer alternated between the various dishes in strict rotation. His expressions while eating were noteworthy; he seemed to enjoy each dish very much, while loathing it a moment later. Nor did the food seem to calm him, for he carried on a whispered monologue between bits.

Hertha listened. The customer was muttering, "I really can't stand the smell of that meat. . . . Yeah, well you can go screw yourself 'cause *I* can't stand the taste of that Chinese slop. . . . What was that? *Your* turn? Loomis, you've already had twice as much as the rest of us. . . ."

Toward the end of the meal the customer's hands were shaking, sweat was dripping from his face, and he seemed ready to go into a full-scale epileptic seizure.

Hertha made her decision, the same decision she always made when confronted by lonely, sick weirdos who nobody else except maybe their mothers would touch with a ten-foot pole.

"Hey," she said, "you look pretty strung out. You got a place to stay?"

The customer left off muttering and looked at her with pain-sick eyes. "Not yet. Could you recommend a quiet hotel?"

"Are you kidding? No place in town would even let you sit in the lobby, the shape you're in. Here." She put a key on the table.

"What's this?"

"It's for my room. You just go to the back of the restaurant and upstairs and it's at the end of the hall. Do you think you can make it?"

Crompton said, "It is very kind of you, but I really don't think . . ." His face contorted dramatically. Then, in a different voice—an attractive, sexy voice—he said, "My dear, this is very good of you. When I am more myself I hope to repay . . ." Again the voice changed. This time it was heavy, husky, hard: "Thanks a lot, lady, I won't make you no trouble."

The customer paid and staggered toward the stairs, clutching the key as though it might open the gates of paradise. Hertha watched him go. The headwaiter also came over and watched.

"Hertha," he said, "what have you gotten yourself into this time?"

She shrugged and laughed, a little nervously.

"What's wrong with that guy, anyhow?" he asked.

"I don't know, Harry. I think maybe he's an out-of-work ventriloquist who's gone off his nut. You should hear the voices he can do!"

35

When Hertha returned to her room that night, she found the man she had befriended sprawled on the floor, delirious. She managed to get him into bed, and she sat in a chair and listened to him raving.

After a while she could make out three different voices coming out of him. Each voice had a name. The three voices talked and argued with each other.

Soon she had their names sorted out. "Crompton" was the one she had met in the restaurant. He seemed to be in charge, though the others were fiercely disputing his leadership. He was uptight, rational, tightly organized, and he spoke in a thin, controlled voice. Then there was "Loomis," who seemed to be an easygoing sort, refined, sophisticated, a ladies' man. He had a light, amusing voice. "Stack" was the third, and he gave the impression of toughness and violence; but there was also something boyish and vulnerable about him. His voice was strong, emotional, compelling.

Sometime they would refer to another man they called "Finch." He evidently was one of them. But he never said a word.

Hertha decided that she liked all three of them,

though in different ways. Crompton was her favorite because he was so pathetic.

Their argument went on interminably. Toward dawn Hertha grew chilly as the mists crept in from the river. The three voices were still going at it. She tried to get into the conversation, but they ignored her. So, after giving the matter due consideration, she got into bed with them.

That took their attention off their quarrel and onto her, at last, and most gratifyingly.

Later, Hertha couldn't decide whether or not what ensued should technically be called an orgy. Whatever it was, it was very good: all of those men seemed to have been without women for a very long time. They were each different: Stack was masculine and loving, Loomis was skillful and amusing, and Crompton, though reluctant at first, was boyish and inexperienced, and sweet.

That afternoon Crompton awoke before the others and explained the situation to Hertha. The orange-haired woman listened quietly as he related the events that had brought them to this condition.

"Wow," she said at last, "that's really something. But now that you're all together in one head, what's supposed to happen?"

"We're supposed to Reintegrate," Crompton said, speaking softly so as not to awaken the others.

"What does that mean?"

"It means we're supposed to become a single, whole individual. But it hasn't happened yet, and it doesn't look like it's going to."

"Isn't there anything you can do?"

Crompton shrugged. "I've tried everything I can think of. My doctor on Earth warned me that there was only a small chance of bringing it off. But I had to try."

"So what'll happen now?"

"I'm afraid that I—we—are going crazy. None of us is able to control the others. I'm supposed to be the most stable of the bunch, and I'm just about at the end of my strength."

"Can't you boys reach some sort of compromise?" Hertha asked.

"We've tried," Crompton told her. "But it never lasts. Not even when we take turns using the body. The conflicts between us simply can't be resolved. Hertha, you have been good to us. Now I want you to leave this room before the others awaken. This time there may be violence."

"Hey, I got an idea," Hertha said. "Why don't you see my psychiatrist. He's done wonders for me."

"It would be useless," Crompton said. "Some of the finest doctors on Earth looked into my case, and they weren't able to do a thing for me."

"Try Dr. Bates anyhow!" Hertha cried. "You can never tell, maybe something new has turned up since you left Earth."

"It's too late," Crompton said. "The others will be waking up soon. This time it will be the final showdown. Frankly, I'm glad it's finally come. I'm just too tired to care anymore."

Crompton's head slumped. His eyes closed and his face grew slack. Then, abruptly, he sat upright. Now his eyes were wide open, unfocused, and his features were set in an expression that Hertha had not seen before.

"Hertha, do not be frightened," a voice said from Crompton's mouth. It was a deep, gentle voice, unlike the others.

"Who are you?" she asked.

"Hertha, you have in your possession a drug called Blue Twilight."

"That's dangerous stuff. How did you know I've got some?"

"Give this body four capsules of it."

"Like hell! That's a strong dose!"

"The drug will not hurt them. In their present state, it will have the effect of a strong soporific."

"It'll put them to sleep? How will that help?"

"The others will sleep; but Crompton is immune to the psychosterazine family to which Blue Twilight belongs. He will be able to maintain sanity and control of the body for a few days longer."

"I know who you are!" Hertha cried. "You're Finch!"

"Give them the drug," the deep solemn voice said. "Tell Crompton I advise him visiting your doctor at once, and taking his advice."

Hertha got the capsules and stuffed four of them into Crompton's mouth. Finch's wide and expressionless eyes did not watch her.

"Why didn't you help them before?" Hertha asked. "Isn't there anything else you can do for them? What sort of person are you, anyhow?"

"I am not a person," Finch said. "I am not even yet a nobody. I have done nothing, and that's something. Maybe you have dreamed all this."

And then Finch was gone.

When Crompton woke up, she told him what had happened.

Crompton shook his head and said, "I don't like it. Finch is there, but he won't talk to us. I don't know what he wants."

"To live, I suppose," Hertha said.

"No, I don't think Finch cares about that. . . . But *I* want to live!"

Hertha's doctor agreed to see Crompton at once.

"Four complete personalities in a single body!" Dr. Bates said, putting away his cognoscope. "That is quite rare, you know, but not unprecedented."

"We can't seem to integrate," Crompton told him. "We can't even cooperate. We're fighting all the time and we're just about at the end of the road. Can you help us?"

"I wish I could," Bates said. "We don't come by this sort of thing very often out here in Ygga. But to be honest, I do not have the resources and equipment that your case requires."

"What do you suggest, then? Should we go back to Earth and look for treatment?"

Bates shook his head slowly. "Your case requires the finest and most advanced techniques available. There is only one place for that. It is quite new, and frankly, experimental. Have you ever heard of Aion Project?"

36

Getting to Aion proved easier than Crompton had anticipated. He had only to take the shuttle from Brenh'a to Yggaville, and then go to the nearest travel agency to book his passage onward. As luck would have it, there was a spaceship leaving for Tung-Bradar that very afternoon, arriving there in time for Crompton to make the Star Valley Connection to Aion.

The journey provided a restful interlude. Crompton became friendly with the ship's drunken Scots android doctor—a fellow crossword fanatic—who provided him with a supply of Blott-44, one of the newer psychosteroids. Through its unique Peripheral Inspread Effect (PIE), Loomis and Stack continued in their deep sleep. Finch showed no response to the drug. But Finch didn't count except as an ominous presence who communicated only his absence.

Crompton, for the first time in many weeks, was the sole and undisputed master of his mind/body. He enjoyed this very much despite the inevitable side effects of the drug—rash on the left side of the nose, greenish saliva, and itchy index fingers.

How blissful, those days in space! Crompton wished he could just go on like this, his own master, all problems suspended indefinitely. But he had been warned: it would only be a matter of days before habituation set in and Loomis and Stack were clamorously with him once more.

He read with care the brochure for Aion that the

travel agency had given him. It was entitled, *Provisional Notes Toward a Paper on Certain Aspects of the Aion Project.*

The Aion Project, snuggled beneath its force dome on the otherwise inhospitable planet Demeter V, is comprised of some ten thousand square miles landscaped to look like California. The result is a green and hospitable land with mountains, valleys, plains, tempting beaches, good restaurants, recreation of every sort, and—of course!—therapies of every description.

All manner of beings come to Aion for assistance, from a bewildering variety of backgrounds and orientations. We try to deal sensitively with all. In our view, all therapies are aspects of a single universal therapy, just as all conscious creatures are aspects of a single Universal Consciousness.

Whether this is true or not, it is a beautiful conception, well worth thinking about.

We at Aion are not formalists, nor are we blind worshippers of academic expertise. We write no textbooks, hold no psychological conferences, and try not to overuse the word *symbol*. We claim no formal knowledge, no special skills, and we utterly repudiate the "guru" role that patients sometimes force on us in their misguided search for an easy path to self-transcendence. In spite of this, perhaps it would not be too paradoxical to state that whatever *can* be done for you, we can do, and whatever *can't* be done for you, we can help you to learn how to do for yourself; and all at competitive rates.

We hope that this clears up some of the more common misconceptions concerning Aion. Let us conclude by saying, "Welcome! You are indeed a lucky sentient creature to have reached so propitious a place as this. Make the best of your opportunity and work diligently to achieve your salvation."

Crompton thought it sounded a little vague, but promising all the same. Anyhow, he was committed. The ship was landing, and Loomis was muttering in his sleep.

37

Crompton went through immigration, health, and customs, and was sent to reception. Here a pretty blond girl in tartan tights helped him fill out his paperwork, collected the fee (200,000 SVUs, nonrefundable), assigned him an apartment, and gave him a map which showed the various features on Aion, including restaurants, boutiques, movie theaters, sex shops, and bowling alleys, also the locations of several hundred ongoing therapies of various sorts, any or all of which he was welcome to join.

"Whatever you want," she told him, "just take, it's all included in the fee. The Center will contact you as soon as you're settled in. Good luck."

"Have you been through the therapy yourself?" Crompton asked.

She shook her head. "They wouldn't accept me. Told me to come back when I had some *real* problems. The bastards! And they talk about compassion! It really bugs me because I know that beneath my apparent placidity and normalcy I am a deeply troubled person. Do you think it shows at all?"

"Not that I can see," Crompton said.

She sighed. "Oh well, I suppose you've got a lot of sick, huh?"

"Well," Crompton said, "I am a paranoid schizophrenic with three different personalities to contend with as well as my own. I guess that's about as sick as they come outside of a funny farm."

"Three different personalities!" she said, looking at Crompton with sudden interest.

"I must admit," Crompton said, "that one of them never says a word and is really no problem. But the other two are a handful."

The receptionist's eyes were glowing and her lips were moist as she murmured, "You're really a Heavy Case, aren't you? I knew it as soon as I saw you. There's a certain aura that the Heavy ones have. . . . By the way, my name is Sue. What about coming up to my apartment tonight and I'll cook dinner and we'll laugh it up and maybe you can give me a few pointers on spotting my disorders. I know that I'm crazy deep down, but I never can get the symptoms straight."

Looking at her eager face and parted lips, Crompton realized that even madness has its ranking order, its heroes, and its groupies. Aion was a place where sickness was the sole industry; so it stood to reason that the real lunatics would be the stars of this culture. It was even probable that an ordinary, garden-variety neurotic would feel outclassed here. After all, your midlife-crisis executive or sexually frustrated housewife wasn't what Aion was all about. No, Aion was for the far-out ones like Crompton with three personalities fighting it out for possession of his body and whatever went with it. *That* was the action of Aion!

Crompton's response was formed by this insight. He said, "Thanks, Sue, I'd really love to do that some other time. But now I've got to get myself sorted out first."

"That's what all the Heavy Cases say," Sue said sadly. "Oh well. Here comes your Two-Hour Friend."

A tall thin black man was approaching. He had a cheerful face and a great head of wiry hair.

"My what?" Crompton asked.

"It is well known," Sue said, "that a Friend is just exactly what a person with heavy psychological difficulties arriving all shook up in a strange place most needs."

"I don't understand."

"So the Aion Foundation provides a Friend for each

incoming guest. The job is on a volunteer basis, but only for two hours at a time since being friends with a person you have nothing in common with and care nothing about is difficult and taxing work."

"Hi," the black man said. "I'm Kavi, I come from Fiji."

"I do not need an assigned Friend," Crompton said. "I really resent—"

"Don't tell it to me," Sue said, "tell it to your Friend. That's what he's there for."

"Tell me all about it, baby," Kavi said, and Crompton let the Fijian lead him outside to a taxi.

38

Kavi helped Crompton settle into a modern one-room apartment on Polyani Boulevard. The place was equipped with an automatic videorecording system that took down every word you uttered and every gesture you made. This was so that patients could monitor their past behavior and thus keep an eye on the progress they were making. Crompton, not untypically, disconnected the apparatus. He wanted to know when the real therapy would begin, and how many hours a day it would require, and what he was supposed to do, and so forth. Kavi told him that there was no fixed procedure.

"You must remember," the good-natured Fijian said, taking a cigarette, lighter, and ashtray out of his voluminous hair and lighting up, "that Aion is the most advanced center for therapeutics that the galaxy has ever known. There is no single therapy or procedure here; instead, a grand eclecticism prevails. In the saying popular here, 'It all depends.' "

"But what does it all depend on?" Crompton asked.

"They never told me that," Kavi admitted.

"What sort of treatment do you get?"

"In my case, a great black raven comes at night and instructs me. Your treatment will probably take some different form, unless you happen to suffer from psychosymbolic ritual pollution, as I do."

"Crompton shook his head. "I'm a paranoid schiz."

"There's quite a few of you lads here," Kavi told him.

By then their two-hour friendship was almost up. They promised to telephone each other in a few days, get together for a drink, and see how the other was getting along. But this in itself was a ritual, since Two-Hour Friends rarely bothered to keep up the relationship, which maybe was part of why they were in the Aion Project.

Crompton spent the rest of the day looking around downtown Aion. He liked the city very much, especially its low pastel buildings set in green parking lots. There were a lot of people around and they all seemed friendly. Most of them were engaged in the group therapy sessions that were continually going on in pizza parlors, movie theaters, hairdressing establishments, and the like. It gave Aion a certain distinctive air, and generated an atmosphere of understanding and compassion that could be felt a hundred miles out in space.

Aion's total preoccupation with therapy and honest communication sometimes made for minor difficulties, as, for example, when Crompton went to a drugstore to get some shaving cream and razor blades.

The clerk, a short bearded man in a check suit, put down his copy of *Inslight*, the Journal of the Midget Psychologists, and asked, "What do you want those things for?"

"To shave with," Crompton replied.

"That's not necessary, you know," the clerk said.

"I know," Crompton said, "but I like to shave."

"Indeed?" The clerk smiled knowingly. "That is a rationalization so obvious that I won't even bother calling your attention to it."

"I don't know what is the matter with you," Crompton said. "Are you going to sell me some shaving cream or aren't you?"

"Don't get excited," the clerk said. "I was merely trying to empathize with your situation via the few clues available to me." He laid out an assortment of shaving creams and razors on the counter. "Take your pick, and don't mind me, I'm just a faceless nobody whose sole function in life is to serve you."

"I didn't mean to insult you," Crompton said. "I was simply trying to get some shaving cream."

"It is apparent to me," the bearded man said, "that you have many important things to do, like shaving your silly face, and that you have no time to spend with a fellow human being who might want to share with you for a fleeting instant the realization that we are something more than our roles, something more than our fleshy envelopes. . . . That we are in fact awareness itself meeting itself in unusual circumstances."

"Is that so?" Crompton replied, and walked out. He could hear applause from the back of the store. It emanated from the bearded man's psychotherapy group.

Crompton saw that people in Aion communicated with each other on the slightest provocation, as if they were all a little drunk and belligerent. Later that afternoon, he was able to watch the Aion style in its fullest flower.

Two cars had had a minor collision at a cross street. The two drivers, obviously unhurt, got out of their cars. Although one was short and stocky and the other lean with a mottled skin, they both resembled account executives in acute midlife crises. They were both smiling.

The tall man surveyed the damage and, in languid, amused tones, said, "The long arm of facticity seems to have brought us to the crunch, so to speak. I wonder if you share with me the perception that you, in the popular expression, *jumped the light*, and hence were responsible for the ensuing mess. I do not want to make you feel guilty, you understand, I am merely trying to establish the facts in as clear, dispassionate, and objective a manner as possible."

There was a murmur of approval from the crowd that had quickly gathered. All eyes were turned expectantly to the short man, who locked his hands behind his back and rocked on his heels in the way Freud is said to have done while considering whether or not there was a death instinct. He said, "Don't you think that pleas based upon the assumption of one's own objectivity are somewhat disingenuous, to say the least?"

The crowd nodded. The tall man said easily, "Granted that all personal judgments are inherently biased. Still, judgment is the only instrument of discrimination at our disposal, and it is our work as living, developing creatures to make discriminations, from which value-judgments inevitably flow. This must be done despite the subjectivity paradox implied in making an 'objective' statement. That is why I say unequivocally that you were in the wrong, and no amount of reference to the observer observed dichotomy is going to change that."

There was a murmur of approval from the crowd. Many of them were taking notes, and a small discussion group had formed at the curb.

The short man knew that he had made a tactical blunder, thereby permitting his opponent to deliver a long speech. He tried desperately to recapture initiative by taking the discussion to another level:

"Don't you ever find your own words a little suspect?" he inquired, with an Iago-like smile. "Have you always had this overwhelming drive to be in the right? How long have you been engineering situations in which *the other* is invariably at fault, thus postponing the moment of facing your primordial and irremedial guilt?"

The tall man, sensing victory, said, "My friend, that is mere psychologizing. You are disturbed by the 'demonic' aspect of your own behavior, I suppose, and are determined to justify it at any cost."

"So now you're a mind reader?" the short man shot back. This drew a murmur from the spectators.

The tall man neutralized this by saying, "I am not a mind reader, my friend, I merely make use of the plentiful sub-cues available to me as to the etiology of your behavior. I think it's pretty obvious to all of us here."

He got a brisk round of applause for that one.

"But damn it," the short man said to the crowd, "can't you see that he's merely playing with words? The concrete evidence puts him in the wrong, no matter what the cost of that insight is to his sense of childlike omnipotence."

The audience muttered their disapproval of that one, and a man whispered to Crompton, "They always trot out the *ad hominem* argument as a last resort, don't they?"

The tall man closed in for the kill. "You wish me to be in the wrong, my poor friend? Very well, I am delighted to be in the wrong if that will be of any assistance to your diseased and deflated psyche. But I would like to point out for your own good that symbolic victories will be of little comfort to you when a time of trial is upon you. No, my good fellow, face up to the real world out there, the pain and sorrow of it all, but yes, the joy, the unutterable bliss of our all-too-brief sojourn upon this green planet!"

There was a moment of hushed silence in which you could hear nothing but the soft hum of many cassette recorders. Then the short man shouted, "Go fuck yourself you fast-talking stupid bastard cunt."

The tall man bowed ironically and the crowd went wild. The short man hastily tried to cover up by pretending that his fit of temper had been an intentional satire upon commonplace behavior. But no one was deceived except perhaps Crompton, who found the entire affair disturbing and bizarre.

When Crompton returned to his apartment, there was a suprex message waiting for him. He was to come to the Intersentient Therapeutics Center at 10:00 A.M. the following morning for his first therapy appointment.

39

The Intersentient Therapeutics Center was a vast collection of buildings of various sizes and shapes, all interconnected by a series of walkovers, flyaways, catwalks, ramps, and other types of architectural integument. The Center was in effect a single gigantic building covering an area of 115.3 square miles. It was one of the largest man-made structures in that sector of the galaxy, coming just after the 207-square-mile used-food center on Opiuchus V.

Crompton passed through the main gate with its famous motto overhead: "A Sound Mind in a Sound Body or Bust." A guard checked him for weapons, and a receptionist verified his appointment and took him to a large, pleasantly furnished office on the second floor. Here he was turned over to Dr. Chares, a small, plump, balding man with gold pince-nez.

"Take a seat, Mr. Crompton," Chares said. "We just have to complete your paperwork, then you can begin treatment. Do you have any questions? Please feel free to ask anything you like: we are here to serve you."

"That's very kind of you," Crompton said. "Would you tell me what is going to happen next?"

Dr. Chares smiled regretfully. "Afraid not. That sort of information would merely precondition your expectations, resulting in the vitiation of your progress and insight. You wouldn't want that to happen, would you?"

"Of course not," Crompton said. "But can you tell me how long the treatment usually takes?"

"That of course depends entirely on you," Chares said.

"Permit me to be blunt. Some exceptional subjects have broken through into health while sitting right there in that chair arranging for their treatment. With others—most of us, I'm afraid—it takes somewhat longer. Ripeness is all, and that's what we're working for here. Beyond that, I would be being less than frank with you if I did not admit that the dynamics of personal health and dynamic growth are still a dimly understood variable, or cluster of interrelated modalities of potential, as I prefer to think of them."

"I think I see what you mean," Crompton said. "Anyhow, you *are* pretty sure you can cure me, aren't you?"

"Our confidence transcends the personal," Chares replied with quiet dignity. "We here at Aion believe that all sentient creatures are endowed with Original Sanity, and that we are the unremitting instrumentalities in the bringing forth of that Sanity. We have never failed, except of course at those times when our anticipations have been frustrated by premature termination of the patient's life processes. Can't win them all, I guess. Is there anything else you'd like to know?"

"I guess you've pretty well covered it," Crompton said.

"Then read this release," Chares said. "It says that you are aware that the course of your therapy may result in death, dismemberment, irreversible insanity, imbecility, impotence, or other undesirable effects. We will take every precaution to avoid those outcomes, of course, but in the unhappy event that one of these eventualities does eventuate, you agree to hold us blameless, and so forth. Just sign at the bottom."

He gave Crompton a replica of a fountain pen. Crompton hesitated.

"That sort of thing hardly ever happens," Chares said encouragingly. "But still, the essence of therapeutic methodology involves real situations with authentic outcomes, and when you play that game you sometimes get unexpected results."

Crompton considered, turning the replica fountain pen in his fingers and thinking how little he liked this setup. His nature rebelled at the idea of putting himself into a situation both ominous and enigmatic, as Aion seemed to him now. He was aware that when they warn you at the

door that you may lose all your marbles inside, you just
might consider looking for a lower-stakes game.

But what alternative did he have? He could feel his
other personality components stirring, cross and argumen-
tative even in their drugged sleep. He was faced with Hob-
son's choice—a crossword puzzle favorite, and an epitome
of his current situation.

Then Loomis, his voice blurry, said, "Al? Whash this?
Whash happening, Al?"

"I'll do it," Crompton said, and hastily scrawled his
signature before he could change his mind.

"That's great," Dr. Chares said, folding the release
and putting it in his breast pocket. "Welcome to the wonderful world of no-shit therapy, Mr. Crompton!"

Crompton's chair suddenly tilted backward, trapping
Crompton in its lap. Then the chair began to descend
through a just-opened hole in the floor.

Crompton called out, "Wait, I'm not ready yet!"

"They never are," he heard Chares say from far above
him.

41

Presently the armchair stopped moving. Crompton stood
up and tested the floor beneath his feet. He found that he
was in a narrow passageway, one side of which was
blocked by the armchair. He began to walk in the other
direction, groping through the darkness with one hand in
contact with the wall.

Loomis woke up and asked, "What's going on, Al? Where are we?"

"That's a little difficult to explain," Crompton said.

"But what's this all about?"

"It's a special therapy we're doing. It's going to make us into a single whole person."

"Walking down a pitch-black tunnel is your idea of therapy?"

"No, no, this is just a preliminary."

"To what?"

"I don't know. They said it was best we didn't know."

"Why did they say that?"

"I'm not sure, I think it's part of the treatment."

Loomis thought about that for a while. Then he said, "I don't understand."

"Well, I don't either," Crompton said. "But that's what they told me."

"I see," Loomis said. "Well, isn't that just great? This is really a nice situation you've gotten us into. You think you're so intelligent, don't you? Let me tell you something, Al, you're not smart, you're stupid."

"Try to be calm," Crompton said. "We are at a very famous and successful place. They know what they're doing."

"It just doesn't look kosher to me," Loomis said. "Can't we just check out of this place and try to sort things out on our own?"

"I think it's a little too late for that," Crompton said. "And anyhow—"

Light, coming from no apparent source, suddenly flooded the corridor. Just ahead, the passageway widened into a large room.

Crompton entered, and saw that he was in a surgical theater. There were tiers of seats, shadowed in gloom. In the center of the room was an elaborate operating table. There were several men standing around the table wearing white coats, rubber gloves, and gauze masks. There was a man lying on the table, his face hidden under a washcloth. In the background, a radio was playing one of last year's top Terran ten, "Tushy Sounds," by Spike Dactyl and the Rump Parliament.

"This looks like it could get unpleasant," Loomis remarked. "I think I'll simply follow my nature and cop out of the action at this point by taking refuge in a meditation on my genitals, a spiritual practice I have been following since childhood."

Stack woke up and said, "What's going on?"

Crompton said, "Quite a lot, but this is hardly the moment for a recapitulation."

"I can fill you in," Loomis said.

"Please do it very quietly," Crompton said. "I've got to cope with this situation." He turned to the doctors. "What is going on here?"

The eldest of the doctors had a long, forked gray beard and an authoritarian manner which he wore with argyle socks, perhaps as an oxymoron of ambiguous intent. He said, "You're late. I trust you are ready to begin now?"

"Begin what?" Crompton said. "I am not a doctor. I don't know what to do."

"It is precisely because you are not a doctor that you have been chosen!" said a short, red-haired doctor from the rear of the group. "We are relying, you see, on your spontaneity and élan."

"Do have a go," another doctor said.

Despite Crompton's protests they dressed him in a surgical gown, slipped rubber gloves over his hands, and tied a gauze mask over his face. Crompton was beginning to feel dizzy and dreamlike. Strange thoughts passed through his mind: Quondam substitutions? Perelmanesque gambit inapropos just now. The intricacy of forgetfulness! And then the peanut butter.

Someone slapped a scalpel into his hand. Crompton said, "If I were to react to this on a reality level, it would be frightening." He unmasked the patient, and beheld a fat-faced man with a mole on his left cheek.

"Gaze well upon him," the fork-bearded doctor said. "Gloat upon your handiwork. Because you and you alone brought him to this as sure as God made little green apples."

Crompton was about to remonstrate, but stopped because just then a pretty red-haired girl clad only in a violet dirndl came into the operating theater and asked, "Is Doctor Groper ready for me yet?"

"No," one of the doctors hissed. He was nondescript except for his voice, which was soft and viscid and hinted at greasy iniquities.

The girl nodded and turned to Crompton. "Wanna see something?"

Crompton was too dumbfounded to respond. But Loomis, who always kept a weather eye open for opportunities like this, broke off explaining the situation to Stack and took over and said, "By all means, my dear, show me something."

The girl reached into a tiny purse which she wore pinned to the waist of her dirndl and took out a pair of silver scissors.

"I never go anywhere without them," she said.

"Never at all? How fascinating," Loomis said. "Why don't we take a walk and you can tell me all about it. I wonder if one can get a drink in this place?"

"Now you must excuse me," the girl said. "I've got to put my toidy to bed." She exited.

"Charming," Loomis murmured, and would have followed her if Crompton had not wrestled back control.

"May we get back to business?" Crompton said icily. He turned to the doctors. "I assume that all of this serves some sort of therapeutic purpose? I *am* the patient around here, am I not?"

"Well, that calls for a bit of explanation," the fork-bearded doctor said, reaching under his mask to scratch what became visible as a harelip.

"I thought you weren't allowed to explain things," Crompton said.

"You misunderstood. We are permitted to explain anything, as long as we don't tell the truth."

"But don't think that simplifies anything for you," said the resident in psychosurgery, who had just come into the room at that moment with his clipboard. "Even our lies contain valuable hints for you to figure out."

"Sometimes a lie and the truth are the same thing," the fork-bearded doctor said. "Anyhow, it's all part of the insight game."

"Do get on with the operation," the resident said, "so we can get away for some lunch."

Crompton looked down at the man on the operating table. He had never seen him before. Various thoughts entered his mind. His left knee had been bothering him lately, and he was irked by the vague sense of having forgotten

something trivial but amusing. He could hear Loomis and
Stack whispering together. It was maddening: that they
should make noise in *his* mind just when he had to oper-
ate! He looked at the scapel in his hand. A wave of doubt
came over him. He tried to remember where he had attended medical school. Instantly he had a picture of the
New Jersey Turnpike at the Cheesquake Bay exit. How
strange the mind was!

He studied a patch of shiny skin between the patient's
eyebrows. Almost absentmindedly he raised the scalpel and
cut deeply.

Instantly he heard the deep whine of a symbol trans-
former in the basement, and the scalpel in his hand
changed into a long-stemmed rose.

Crompton suffered then a momentary syncope. When
he had recovered, the patient, doctors, operating theater,
indeed, the whole construct, had faded.

Now he was standing in a formal garden on a high
cliff that overlooked a wrinkled blue sky.

40

Once it must have been a beautiful garden, with its formal
walks and meanders. But now it was sadly overgrown. The
purple verbena was still doing nicely, and the notch-eared
kalanchoes looked eminently prosperous; but dandelions
were now blooming everywhere, and a barrel cactus had
taken up residence near the gazebo. The grounds were covered with dog turds, tin cans, newspapers, and rusted
camping equipment.

Crompton noticed that he was holding a long-handled rake in one hand, a shovel in the other. He knew what he had to do. Humming to himself, he raked debris into neat piles, picked up funk and crap, and even found time to prune a few rosebushes. He felt good doing this.

But then he noticed that a black and evil-smelling blight had sprung up behind him. There were patches of rot wherever he had stepped.

The sky darkened, a bitter wind whipped through the garden, and black clouds scudded by overhead. A heavy rain commenced to fall, transforming the garden into an instant bog. And, as if that weren't enough, deafening thunderclaps shook the garden, and forked bolts of lightning lit up the livid sky.

A holocaust of black flies swept in, followed by a procession of long-snouted Peruvian weevils with their tiny tan parasites. These in turn were followed by vultures and iguanas, and the ground beneath Crompton's feet commenced to tremble, to crack, to heave in vast sluggish ripples.

A fissure opened in the ground, and in its depths Crompton could see the sulfurous glow of hellfires.

"Now really," Crompton said, "what is this all about?"

There was a moment of uncanny silence. Then a great voice that seemed to come simultaneously from all parts of the sky called out. *"Daniel Stack! This is the hour of your reckoning!"*

"But wait a minute," Crompton said, "I'm not Stack, I'm Crompton."

"So where's Stack?" the voice bellowed.

"He's here, but this is *my* therapy, not his!"

"I don't know nothing about that," the vast voice retorted. "I got an order to deliver an hour of reckoning to Daniel Stack. Do you want to accept it for him?"

"No, no," Crompton said. "I've got my own problems. Just a moment, I'll get him."

Crompton turned his gaze inward. "Dan?"

"Leave me alone," Stack said. "I'm practicing introspection."

"There's someone here wants to speak to you."

"Tell them to go away," Stack said.

"Tell them yourself," Crompton said, and dived down

into his own unconscious for a brief and well-deserved nap.

Stack reluctantly took over the body and its various sensoria. "Yeah, what is it?"

"Daniel Stack!" the great voice from the sky bellowed. "This is the time of your reckoning. I am the spokesman for the men you have murdered. Do you remember them, Dan? There was Argyll, Lanigan, Lange, Tishler, and Wey. They have been waiting a long time for this moment, Dan, and now—"

"What was that last name?" Stack asked.

"Wey. Charles Xavier Wey."

"I never killed anybody by that name," Stack stated. "The others, yes. Wey, no."

"Could you have forgotten?" the voice enquired.

"Are you kidding? Do you think I'm blasé or something, not to remember who I've killed. Who is this Wey and why is he trying to hang a bum rap on me?"

There was a brief silence broken only by the hiss of rain falling into the fiery fissure. Then the voice said, "The case of Mr. Wey will be looked into later. But now, Dan Stack, here are your dead come to greet you!"

Again there was silence. Then an irritable voice from somewhere could be heard to say, "All right, black out the garden set. Christ, isn't anyone on the ball around here?"

Then there came darkness of a density like unto infinite layers of marmoset fur.

42

Alarmed by the proceedings, Crompton took over control of the body again from Stack. Crompton saw that he was standing in a large, high-ceilinged room painted buff and brown, with tall thin windows and a subtle aroma of legality. A placard at the rear read: SUPERIOR COURT OF KARMIC INSTRUMENTALITY, SECTION VIII, JUSTICE O. T. GRUDGE PRESIDING. It looked like any American small-town courtroom: rows of wooden benches for spectators and interested parties; tables and chairs for lawyers, plaintiffs, defendants, and witnesses. The judge's bench was raised to dominating height, and to its right was the witness stand.

The bailiff called out, "All rise."

Justice Obadiah Grudge came in briskly, a small, middleaged man, mostly bald, with rosy cheeks and glinty blue eyes. "Sit down, if you please," he said. "We are today considering the case of Daniel Stack, a sentient being whose loose ends are presently to be tied up, if I may be permitted the colloquialism, in a manner appropriate and peculiar to the Law of Causality as it is commonly understood in this corner of the galaxy. Come forward, Mr. Stack."

Crompton said, "I am appearing for him, your honor. He is an aspect of my personality, my ward, as you people would understand if you looked over the details of the case. As such he cannot be considered a discrete individual in his own right. Stack is not in fact a proper person or personage as defined by common usage in the school of hard knocks, if I may be permitted the analogy. He is a mere aspect of a greater personality; of msyelf, with all modesty, from whom he became detached due to circumstances beyond our control. Hence it is our contention that 'Daniel Stack' cannot be tried as an individual since his individualism so-called is merely a facet of myself, to whom he stands in the relationship of shadow to object, if I may coin a phrase."

The judge asked, "Are you putting yourself forward, Mr. Crompton, to stand for Stack's alleged crimes?"

"In no way, your honor! I, Alistair Crompton, have committed no such crimes, therefore I could not be tried for them even if I so wished. But I maintain that Stack cannot be tried either, for the reasons of nonindividuality previously stipulated, and because he has no body peculiar to himself upon which punishment could be visited."

"No body?" asked Judge Grudge.

"None, your honor. Stack's own body has perished. He is a temporary lodger in the body of myself. Alistair Crompton. I am in the process of integrating myself, which might be viewed as a sentence of death upon whatever meager individualism Stack possesses, since he will cease to exist thereafter except as a symbolically manifested aspect of myself. Since Stack's body has perished and his personality will soon cease to exist. I plead habeas corpus: there is no mind or body here answerable for the alleged crimes of Daniel Stack."

The judge chuckled. "That's a clutch of pretty arguments, Mr. Crompton. But I need not even consider them, for they are beside the point. The most interesting consideration you raise is the question of what is part of something else and what is discrete, complete and competent in itself. But that is merely a philosophical question. The legal position is quite clear, and has been established by precedents too numerous to cite. Suffice it to say that, legally, everything may be considered complete and entire on one level, yet part of something else on another level. Therefore your position, or mine, is qualitatively no different from Dan Stack's. We are all responsible for what we do, Mr. Crompton, no matter how minuscule our qualifications to uniqueness and wholeness."

"But your honor, where does that leave me? I am in the unfortunate position of sharing my body with Stack.

Therefore any judgment passed upon him will be visited
also—and most unfairly—upon me, as well."

"That's the human situation, Mr. Crompton," the
judge said gently.

"But I am innocent of Stack's alleged crimes. It is fundamental to the tradition of jurisprudence from which we
both spring that the innocent shall not suffer with the
guilty, even at the cost of freeing the guilty!"

"But you are not innocent," Judge Grudge pointed
out. "You are responsible for Stack, and he for you."

"But how can that be, your honor? We were physically and mentally separated when Stack was doing his alleged crimes."

"Schizophrenia is no excuse under karmic law," the
judge stated. "All aspects of a common mind/body are responsible for each other. Or to put it in simpler language,
the left hand is liable to punishment when the right hand
steals the jam."

"Exception," Crompton said.

"Overruled," the judge said. "Let Stack come forth
and the trial begin."

43

Crompton relinquished control. Stack took over.

"Daniel Stack?" the judge asked.

"Yes, your honor," Stack said.

"Here are your accusers." The judge gestured at a
bench directly in front of him. Upon that bench sat four
men who looked like they had been in a major car accident
about five minutes ago. They were bloody and wounded,

and they looked pretty grim about it, just like in a horror movie.

Stack walked over to the bench. Accused and accusers looked each other over. Then Stack nodded in greeting, and the others nodded back.

"Well now," Stack said, "I never thought I'd be seeing you fellows quite so soon. How you been keeping?"

Abner Lange, the oldest of the victims, said, "We're okay, Dan. What about yourself?" He spoke with difficulty due to the ax blow that had staved in his face.

"Well, I'm in a peculiar situation," Stack said. "But it'd take me too long to tell you about it. We might as well get down to business. Do you boys have some complaint against me?"

The men on the bench looked at each other uneasily. Then Abner Lange said, "Well, Dan, we're here on account of you killed us. We are the inescapable consequences of your actions, and therefore we constitute a major portion of your undischarged karma. That's what they told me it was about, but I don't claim to completely understand it."

"I don't understand it at all," Stack said. "Just what is it you fellows want?"

"Well, hell," Lange said, "I don't know. They just told us to come down here and speak our piece."

Stack rubbed his chin. He was genuinely perplexed. He couldn't think of anything to do for these fellows. He said, "Well, boys, what can I tell you? That's the way it is."

One of the victims, Jack Tishler, a tall man with a bullet hole obliterating most of his nose, said, "Goddamit, Dan, maybe it's none of my business but I do believe that you're supposed to show repentence or something like that."

"Well, sure," Stack said. "I'm sorry. I do apologize for having killed you fellows."

"I don't think that is quite what they had in mind," Lange said. "A man kills a man, he ought to say something more than a mealymouthed 'sorry.' And anyhow, you're not sorry, are you?"

"No, I'm not," Stack admitted. "I was just trying to be polite. Can you give me one good reason why I should *actually* feel sorry?"

The victims thought for a while. Then Roy Argyll

said, "Well, there's the matter of our widowed women and orphaned children. How about them, Dan?"

Stack grinned and said, "You'll be talking about your heartbroken third cousins and pet hound dogs next. You fellows never gave a damn about all that when you were alive. Why are you so concerned now?"

"He's got a point," Jim Lanigan remarked to Abner Lange.

"Dan always was a good talker," Lange said.

Stack asked, "Would any of you give a damn if it was you that killed me?"

"Sheet no," Abner Lange said, "I'd be happy to do it for you now, if only I could!"

Stack turned to the judge. "Well, there's where it's at, your honor. I've always maintained that murder should be properly understood as a crime without a victim, since nobody gives a damn before or after and it's mostly a matter of luck who kills and who gets killed. So I respectfully submit that I fail to see what all the fuss is about and I move that we have a couple of drinks together and forget the whole business."

"Mr. Stack," Judge Grudge said, "you exhibit a moral obtuseness that makes me want to fwow up, if I may be permitted the colloquialism."

"Well, your honor," Stack said, "meaning no disrespect, I beg to differ with you about my so-called moral obtuseness. From my viewpoint *you* are morally effete due to the exaggerated and disproportionate importance you give to how sentient creatures die. You're kidding yourself, judge; we all have to go and it don't make much difference how we do it. And besides, who are you to sit in judgment over another man's code of values and sense of the appropriate?"

"I de judge," the judge said pleasantly. "That's how come I get to sit up here and pass judgment on you, Dan. I want to tell you that it has been interesting to hear your obvious rationalizations; and your feeble flights into discursive philosophy have given me something to giggle about later with my friends at the Righteousness Club. It remains only my not unenjoyable task to pass sentence upon you."

Stack stood firm and erect, his eyes fiercely fixed upon the judge's. He folded his arms, displaying scorn.

"Und zo," the judge said, "having heard all of the evidence and having weighed and considered it in my mind, I render now the following verdict: that you will be taken from this place to a place of punishment, and there you shall be hung upside down over a cauldron of boiling yak turds and forced to listen to Franck's Symphony in D Minor played on a kazoo until the karmamometer shows that all your seeds are cooked and that you are in a good state of acculturation."

Stack staggered back, a look of horror on his face. "Not the kazoo!" he pleaded. "How in God's name did you find out about the kazoo?"

"Not for nothing are we the acknowledged masters of psychological methodology," the judge said. "For passing along that little gem of a concealed phobia we are indebted to Mrs. Martha Stack. Stand up and take a bow, Martha!"

Stack's foster-mother stood up in the back of the courtroom and waved her umbrella. Her hair had been hennaed and teased for the occasion.

"Ma," Stack cried, "why did you do it?"

"It's for your own good, Dan'l," she said. "I'm right happy to help you toward redemption, and these good people said that little details such as that could help them reach the soft, loving, God-fearing core that we all know is within you struggling to get out."

"Christ," Stack said, grinding his teeth, "I had forgotten what a dummy you are."

"Well, I do apologize if I've caused you any difficulties," Mrs. Stack said. "At least they don't know about the lace knickers and the little plastic watering can."

"Ma!"

Mrs. Stack said, "I am well-meaning but clumsy. It has been that way for me since childhood. Let me tell you a touching little anecdote—"

"Some other time," said Judge Grudge. "Bailiffs! Come carry this lout away to his just torments!"

Four burly men in waterproof glen-plaid business suits came through a side door and seized Stack. Crompton was fighting to take over control of the body long enough to lodge a plea of insanity. (If all else failed, he was planning to go insane. Crompton didn't mind the kazoo, but he did have a deep-set phobia against being suspended upside down over a cauldron of boiling yak turds.)

At this precise moment the sound of a gong could be heard, shocking in its piercing sweetness.

44

The double doors at the entrance to the courtroom swung open. In marched a procession of silver-robed priests with shaven heads and intaglio begging bowls. To the solemn accompaniment of timpani and celestia they chanted obscure and deep-throated mantras until they reached the judge's bench. Here they stopped and made deep genuflections of an unearthly intricacy and grace. This complete, the most venerable of them stepped forward.

He nodded to the judge.

He bowed to Dan Stack!

"Welcome, welcome, thrice welcome, O Avatar," the venerable priest said to Stack. "We of the Immanent Brotherhood want to take this opportunity of thanking you for all the trouble you've gone to going into manifestation for us. It was really extremely kind of you. We are aware that it is all part of your bodhisattva vow, and predestined anyhow, but we want you to know that we really do appreciate it."

"Hunh," Stack said, noncommittally.

"We have prepared a very nice room for you at the temple, despite your greatly respected indifference to such things. As for food, we know that you are perfectly content with whatever we give you, or nothing at all, which makes it difficult for us to arrange pleasing menus for you. But we will do our best. You will find that the affairs of humans haven't changed much since your last incarnation on Earth. Same game, different players."

Judge Grudge intervened at this point. "Now look here, padre, I don't mean any disrepect of religion, and I know that you people have your own way of doing things. But it so happens that that fellow you call an avatar is a guilty convicted cold-blooded murderer and I just thought you might want to know that."

"Ah," said the venerable priest, "is misunderstanding. Good joke!"

"I fail to get it," the judge said.

"This person Daniel Stack," the priest said, "is not the being we have come here to honor. Oh, no! Stack is merely the vehicle, the outer shell through which the Avatar will soon burst. . . ."

"That should be all right," the judge said. "It sounds even more final than yak turds."

Crompton managed to gain control of the body at this point. "Now look," he said, "you've got this all wrong. First of all, it isn't Stack's body. It's *my* body. I am Alistair Crompton, and I am trying to integrate my personality components."

"We know all about you," the priest said. "Our Wise Ones, in their caves in Tibet and their A-frames in California, have previewed the entire sequence. We have sympathized with the misplaced obsessive emotionality you have thrown into your delusional activities."

"What do you mean, 'delusional'? I know what I'm doing!"

The priest shook his head gently. "Whatever you think is wrong. I suppose you feel that you live your own life and strive to achieve your goals?"

"Well, of course!"

"But that is not the case at all. Actually, you have no independent life of your own. You do not live, you are lived! You are a completely automatic mechanism with a built-in I-reflex. Your life has no meaning, since you are not even a person. You are nothing more than a short-lived, inconsistent, and accidental collection of tendencies. Your only possible relevance is as the unwitting vehicle for the purpose of bringing forth the Avatar."

"Who is this Avatar? You're not talking about Loomis, are you?"

"You and Loomis and Stack are stages of development, nothing more. You have been brought together as it was directed eons ago in the Codicil to the Secret Documents of Mankind, for the sole purpose of bringing forth the bodhisattva Maitreya whom you know under the terrestrial name of Barton Finch."

"Finch!" Crompton cried. "But he's a moron!"

"That shows how much you know about it," the priest said.

"You're really serious about this?"

"Entirely so."

"You really claim that the whole point of my life has been to bring Finch into the world?"

"That's beautifully put," the priest said. "And you will be honored as an immediate precursor of the superman. Your own personality has served its cosmic purpose now, which should come as a great relief to you. Now you may rest, Crompton, you and Loomis and Stack, for your karmic obligations are discharged and you have won freedom from the cycle of suffering and rebirth, pleasure and pain, hot and cold. You are released from the Wheel of Life! Isn't that great?"

"What do you mean?" Crompton asked suspiciously.

"I mean that you have achieved Nirvana."

"And what is Nirvana?" Crompton demanded.

There was a stirring in the ranks of priests and disciples when he said this, for rarely does anyone get a chance to demonstrate his esoteric understanding by being given a direct question like this, unlike in the old Zen days when there were plenty of straight men around.

"Nirvana," one of the priests remarked, "is the bunion on my little toe."

"No," another said, "actually, Nirvana is everything except the bunion on your little toe."

"Why do you make it so complicated?" another priest said. "Nirvana is simply what's left over when you drain away the water."

Others were ready with their own suggestions, but a short and rather venerable priest held up his hand for silence, then broke wind loudly. Four disciples went into instant samhadi. It seemed conclusive until another short but respectfully venerable priest grumbled, "There's less here than meets the nose."

"It is not easy to explain Nirvana," the original interlocutor-priest said to Crompton. "It can't be dealt with in words at all, you know, which makes precision difficult. Let's just say that you won't feel a thing and you won't even be aware that you won't be feeling a thing."

"I don't like it," Crompton said immediately.

"Now lookee here," the judge said to Crompton, "it appears to me that you're not taking a very positive attitude toward all this. Here is this religious gentleman who has very kindly offered you Nirvana in return for hatching his god or devil or ju-ju or whatever this Finch is, and you start carrying on like he's doing something terrible to you."

"This Nirvana," Crompton said, "sounds just like being stone-cold dead."

"Well, give it a try," the judge said, "maybe it won't be so bad."

"If it sounds so good, why don't you try it?"

"Because I'm not worthy," the judge said. "Where is this Finch, anyhow? I'd like to get his autograph for my son. It's hard to find a nice present for a twenty-two-year-old boy who has taken a vow of poverty and is now living in a cave in Bhutan."

"By the way," the venerable priest said, "I forgot to mention that with Nirvana you also get complete and unexcelled Enlightenment."

"Hey now," the judge said, "that's really something!"

"I don't want Enlightenment!" Crompton shouted.

"That," one of the priests remarked to another, "is Enlightenment indeed."

The priest said, "Let's quit horsing aound. Let the ceremony begin!"

There was a flourish of hautboys. Radiance filled the air. Swarms of ethereal beings came from the four corners of the universe to greet the newly emerging bodhisattva. The tattva gods were there, of course, and there came Thor, Odin, Loki, and Frigg, disguised as Swedish tourists having unhappy love affairs. And there was Orpheus in chicano silk shirt and levis, playing his electric charango via an AC source in his thumos. Quetzalcoatl showed up with his feather boa, Damballa came in his necklace of skulls, and there were many others.

They crowded the room, a spiritual convocation of such enormous power that even the furniture and fittings took on quasi-human characteristics, and a turkey-red curtain could be heard remarking to the portrait of Washington, "I only wish my Uncle Otto could be here to see all this."

"And now," said the priest to Crompton, "if you would be good enough to withdraw your pseudopersonality and allow Finch to come through—"

"Not a chance," Crompton snarled. "If Finch is so great let him find his own body. I'm keeping this one."

"You're ruining the whole production," the priest told him. "Can't you think of anyone but yourself? Don't you realize that everything is of a suchness?"

Crompton shook his head. There was a moment of silence broken only by the wheezing of the air conditioner.

Then a gigantic presence formed in the middle of the courtroom.

Black it was and many-headed, and its shoes were number nine, and it had a midshape somewhat resembling a snake who has swallowed a goat whole. A silvery radiance gleamed from its ebony limbs, at the terminations of which depended tentacles gripping a great variety of edged and toothed weapons.

"I am Thagranak," the baleful presence proclaimed. "Know ye that now the three moons of Kyuuth are aligned with the great constellation of the Greptzer, and the double-nosed worshippers of the Polka Dot Abomination demand blood as a Faigh-gift of our ancient Arrangement. Thus it is that I come via contingencies too fleeting to be imagined to perform the Death upon the Selected One."

"Who is this being?" the venerable priest remarked to a shorter priest.

The shorter priest quickly glanced through a microfilm printout of Smith's Shorter List of Galactic Presences which had been astrally projected to him from the ever vigilant Deity Analyzer and Tabulator (DAT) in Lhassa. "I don't find any mention of him."

"Could he be an imposter?" the venerable priest mused. "No, I suppose not. So he must be from some other universe. That's the usual explanation for the inexplicable."

"But should we admit him to this assembly?" the

shorter priest asked. "He seems rather crude and anthropo-morphic and not our sort of being at all."

"What's there to do? Out-of-universe deities always have visiting privileges at our get-togethers. Anyway, he solves a problem for us."

"Ah so?"

"Even so. Crompton refuses to merge his fictitious ego with the quintessential extinction that the attainment of Nirvana implies, and so make way for the bodhisattva Finch. We ourselves are men of dispassion and so cannot force Crompton to snuff out, no matter how badly we would like to. But here, synchronistically, this archetypi-cally male deity comes to do the job for us. It's neat, isn't it? Thagranak, do it!"

45

At this point there took place a transition of great color, speed, and efficacy. Gone were the solemn priests, the quizzical judge, the awesome extra-universal deity, the courtroom and all its homely accoutrements. For a mo-ment there was nothing at all except vistas of the small glimmering gunmetal cubes that are the fundamental build-ing blocks of reality. Then these too were gone, leaving behind only a thin dusty dream-substance. This coalesced, grew horns and headlights, and turned into a place that looked just like Ming the Merciless's secret control room deep in the bowels of the invisible planet Xingo.

Crompton stood within the room, struggling for com-prehension.

Presently a man entered. Even though the man was dressed in orange leotards and a fright wig, Crompton would have known him anywhere.

"John Blount!"

"Surprised to see me, are you, Crompton? I have watched with amusement your futile twistings and turnings across the galaxy. So near and yet so far, eh, Crompton? Hee hee hee!"

"How did you manage to kidnap me like this?" Crompton demanded. "The Center is sure to make inquiries."

"I doubt it," Blount said. "You see, I have leased the Aion Project for twenty-four hours, and everybody must do as I say."

"The directors of the Center won't let you kill me! They are philosophers, humanitarians. This is against everything they stand for!"

"But they have to stand for it," Blount said. "You see, I took the precaution of also leasing their professional ethics and personal morality for twenty-four hours."

"Gawwwkr," Crompton said.

"I set my trap a long time ago, Alistair. My agents, disguised as grooks, colonels, confidence men and waitresses, have kept in constant contact with you, and have even given you a helping hand now and then. Why not? I was glad to help you to Aion—and me!"

"You really do hold a grudge for a hell of a long time," Crompton remarked.

"My grudge feeds and nourishes me," Blount said. "It has given me a new interest in life, even offered a fresh field for my talents. I am much beholden to you, Crompton. Without you, I would never have discovered the true meaning and purpose of my life."

"That purpose, it seems, is simply to have revenge on me."

"There is that, of course. But that is only the beginning. Crompton, there's so much more!"

"I don't understand."

"Are you a religious man, Crompton? No, I suppose not. I can hardly expect you to understand the terrible beauty of what happened to me one fateful day, when I was reminding myself, as usual, 'Don't forget to have your revenge on Crompton.' "

"Well, what did happen?"

"Suddenly I heard a great voice in my head, and it seemed to come from nowhere and from everywhere, and I fell to my knees because I knew at once that this was the Real Thing. And the Voice said to me, 'Johnikins!' (calling me by a name only my deceased grandmother had used!) 'Johnikins, what will you do *after* you have revenged yourself on Crompton?' I said, 'Well, I'll probably need a vacation after that, so maybe I'll buy Portugal for a few weeks.' And the Voice said to me, 'That's pretty small potatoes, Johnikins.' And I said, 'I know, Lord, it's really pretty banal, isn't it? Here I am, the richest, smartest, and most powerful man in the universe, and all I have to do with my life is get revenge on Crompton, and after that I've got nothing at all. Tell me, Voice, what should I do?' And the Voice said, 'It's so obvious, Johnikins: after you're done with Crompton, why not take your revenge on *the rest of them?*'

"It was as if a great light had turned on in the middle of my brain, and I fell on my face and laughed and cried and praised the Lord. It was the only spiritual revelation I have ever had."

Here Blount paused to take a sip of water.

"The more I thought about it, the more I saw how right the Voice had been. Yes, why not take my revenge on all the people who had ever contributed to my discomfort! It was an exhilarating idea and I sat down at once to make up a list. But there were just too many people. I saw that it would be easier to think in categories. And so I determined to do away with all headwaiters and taxi drivers, pop singers and policemen, car-park attendants and roller derby entrepreneurs, farmers and mixing dubbers, folk singers, dopers, lawyers, Albanians, baseball players . . . I could go on and on."

"I'm sure you could, and will," Crompton said.

"I saw that it would save a lot of time if I just decided what categories I did *not* want to kill. I thought about it and realized that there weren't any. For a while I thought of saving the spotted Dalmatians because I was raised by one. But even they can be a pain in the ass. In a flash of insight I saw that I hated everybody and everything. That simplified my problem. I saw at once what I had to do. I'm sure you know what I mean."

"Do you mean what I think you mean?" Crompton asked.

Blount considered the question. "What do you think I mean?"

I think that you are seriously planning to destroy all of mankind."

"That's it! That's precisely it! And womenkind too, of course. And animalkind. I'm going to destroy all of the kinds—because none of them is worth diddly shit."

"You're crazy!" Crompton gasped.

"Get me out of here!" Loomis wailed.

Dan Stack suddenly entered the discussion. "Let's keep our cool," he said, exuding a strong air of confidence. "This looks like the sort of situation for yours truly. I'll take over now."

Crompton did not resist. Dan Stack took control of the body.

46

"Well," Stack said, "it's an ambitious scheme, all right, and a damned good one if I'm any judge."

Blount was surprised. "Why—thank you very much! I had thought, in your situation—"

"Look," Stack said, "no matter what my situation, I can still appreciate artistry. And you've got it, baby."

"Do you really feel that?" Blount asked. "You don't think I'm crazy?"

"Crazy like a fox," Stack said, winking. "It's exactly what I'd do in your spot, and I'm not crazy, am I?"

"Certainly not!" Blount said. "So you really like my plan?"

"I love it!" Stack said. "How are you planning to begin?"

"I've got an initial sequence drawn up," Blount said proudly.

Crompton managed to regain control long enough to shout, "No, I refuse to be a party to this. I won't let you do this!"

"Is anything the matter?" Blount asked.

"No," Stack said. "That wasn't me, that was Crompton."

"Aren't *you* Crompton?"

"Certainly not. I'm one of the other personalities. I'm Dan Stack."

"Oh! Pleased to meet you. It's hard to realize . . . I mean you look just like . . . I'm John Blount, of course."

"I know all about you," Stack said. "I've been browsing through Crompton's memory files."

"Then you know what he did to me."

"I know. And it really was not very nice of him," Stack said. "But of course, he's really not a nice person. God knows, he's caused me nothing but trouble and grief ever since he talked me into going in with him."

"I can well imagine," Blount said. "You know, Dan, I like you. It would be nice to have you around—if that suited you."

"Suits me just fine," Stack said.

"I've got no one to talk to about my work, you see."

"It's a lonely job, destroying mankind," Stack observed.

"But we must get rid of that Crompton fellow!"

"My sentiments, exactly. I think we can figure something out." He chuckled. "And as long as we're at it, let's do for Loomis, too. He's not worth diddly shit."

"You've got an interesting mind," Blount said, shaking Stack's hand in both of his. "It's going to be a pleasure working with you. Now let's go to my War Games Room and initiate Plan Lettra Destructicon. This is the plan in which I eliminate all of the postmen on Earth. I've had enough of them withholding my important letters."

"Beautiful," Stack said. "Let's go."

47

Just at this moment there was a break in the continuity. It began with a shimmering and a trembling and a shaking. Then clouds of yellowish smoke appeared and coalesced into koala bears that scampered under the furniture. Next the walls began to bubble and sing, and the chairs flashed on and off.

These were the forewarnings of the dreaded REALITYQUAKE, which alters everything, usually for the worst.

The room metamorphosed into the Roman Forum, the Traitor's Tower, Trader Vic's in San Francisco, a Stucky's pecan emporium on U.S. 301 in Georgia, and finally settled down as a Greek Revival room copied loosely from 2001.

In this room, seated around a large redwood table, were a group of men wearing cowboy hats and black silk masks.

A man in a slate-blue sharkskin suit and tennis shoes entered briskly from a concealed doorway on the left. It was Secuille!

"Gawkkkr," Blount said, ashen-faced.

"Yes," Secuille said, "the time of reckoning is at hand, Blount. Assembled here is the Committee for the Preservation of the Story Integrity. Perhaps they are better known to you as the *Archetype Vigilantes*."

"My God, no!" Blount said.

"Blount, you really ought to be ashamed of yourself. Nobody is interested in your crummy *Weltanschauung*.

This is Crompton's story, and you are only a bit player in it."

"Well, hell," Blount said, "a character's got a right to improve himself, hasn't he?"

Secuille turned to the Vigilantes. "Gentlemen, I think you can see that Blount has egotistically violated the situational premise and thus deflected the story into an unwanted and unprofitable channel."

One of the Vigilantes said, "Yep, it's clear enough. I reckon we'd better just write him out."

Another Vigilante said, "How would you like to go, Blount? Car accident? Massive coronary? Sleeping pills?"

"Please don't write me out!" Blount pleaded. "I'm sorry, I repent, I'll never do it again!"

Secuille said, "I wonder if we can trust you. . . ."

"I'll be good! You'll see! You'll be proud of me!"

"Hmmm. . . ."

Blount waited no longer. Sensing that he was being given an inferential opportunity to escape being written out, he quickly converted all of his assets into cash, gave that away to the poor, and retired to the same cave in Bhutan which housed Otto Grudge, the son of Judge O. T. Grudge. In later years Blount became known as the Weird Monk because of his habit of counting his teeth in public. He plays no further part in this story.

"Secuille, I don't know how to thank you," Crompton said. "Is there any way I can help you in your Game?"

Secuille said, "You have already helped me, Crompton, by getting into this ridiculous situation from which I have extricated you, thus winning five hundred red points for three clear overs. How about that?"

"I'm so glad," Crompton said.

"Well, I'll be seeing you." Secuille folded the Vigilantes into a large brown manila envelope and started toward the door.

"Wait!" Crompton cried.

"Yes, what is it?"

Crompton said. "What do I do now?"

"How should I know? It's your story. I'm just a subsidiary character of no great relevance."

"Secuille, please! I simply can't go on like this anymore!"

"There's really only one thing left to do," Secuille

said. "You boys are just going to have to fight it out until Reintegration takes place, or until one of you succeeds in assimilating the others."

"We've been fighting continuously ever since we met." Crompton said. "All it's doing is driving us crazy."

"That's because you've been doing it the bad, old-fashioned way, the way of internalized conflict. But now, modern science has devised a good, easy, up-to-date method of externalizing your innermost conflicts, and thus quickly resolving them."

"How?" Crompton asked.

"By taking advantage of the Aion Foundation's ultimate therapeutic weapon—the External Conflicts Simulator."

"And what, pray tell, is that?"

"The External Conflicts Simulator is a device which projects you into a metaphorized space-time construct. You are then free to simulate weaponry and allies to the best of your abilities. It's as simple as that."

"Huh?" Stack said.

"To put it even more simply—it projects you into a nescient situation where you can fight out your objectivized dream-wars to the death."

"Oh," Stack said.

"It's equivalent to a classical dueling situation, but in this case, metaphorized weapons-systems are utilized. This allows each of you to fight with the conceptual weapons most appropriate to his skills and strengths. The outcome, I am happy to say, will leave only one of you in sole possession of the Crompton Corpus."

"I still do not really understand what we are to do," Crompton complained.

"I'm afraid I don't have the time to give you an introductory course in simulation theory," Secuille said. "Don't worry, you'll pick it up as you go along. What do you say, fellows?"

"I say let's do it," Stack said.

"Fine by me," Loomis said.

"All right," Crompton said.

Even Finch contributed a nuance of agreement.

"Then it's up up and away!" Secuille said.

Discontinuity set in like bleed-pictures end-projected

onto dissolving filmstrips. Crompton wanted to ask a few more questions, but he found himself falling endlessly through a gray featureless void and he knew that the end had begun at last.

48

The word *parameters* was echoing senselessly in his mind. Crompton looked and saw that he was nowhere. It was a strange and uncanny experience, for in this nowhere there was *nothing at all*; not even Crompton himself.

The problem of describing "nothingness" has haunted writers for centuries. It was not as though Crompton were merely present without anything around him, like a man falling through space. *That* would be easy enough to describe. But in this case, not only was there nothing surrounding Crompton, there was also no person there to be surrounded. There was nothing. There was *only* nothing. And yet, something in this nothing was aware, and this awareness Crompton called "I," even though it might have been anyone, or even a property of the nothingness itself.

At first it was a good experience: the nonexistence of himself and everything else was fun, like schussing down a million-mile ski run. But presently Crompton grew frightened. Speed kills, doesn't it? And when you kill nothing, that leaves you with nothing doubled, a truly disastrous position.

Monism was nice, but Crompton saw that he was going to have to get into duality. He experimented cautiously by creating light. That worked out well. Next he needed something to look at, so he simulated the first thing that came to mind—a small teak coffee table. It looked so strange hanging there in nothingness that Crompton quickly simulated a chair, and then he simulated himself and sat down in the chair.

Everything felt more normal once he had a body. But it just wasn't good enough to be a unique and solitary body sitting at a coffee table in the midst of nowhere. It didn't really get him anywhere. So he created the Earth as quickly and neatly as possible.

After a short rest he surveyed his handiwork. He saw that he had gotten the North American coastline all bulgy and wrong, and his oak trees resembled dwarf mandarins. There were many other anomalies. It was not a godlike effort, but at least it gave him something to look at.

He was feeling lightheaded and silly now and he couldn't remember what he was supposed to do next. So he created a place where he could get some lunch and await further developments. This place was Maplewood, New Jersey, in the year 1944. It was the only town on the face of the metamorphized Earth at that time, and Crompton brought to it a rule of equanimity and peace that will long be remembered in the illusory annals of the state.

It was a lazy, good-natured time of long golden autumn afternoons, fading to deep twilight, and then proceeding directly to dawn. Crompton hadn't mastered linear time yet. In Maplewood it was forever October 1, and might have continued forever that way with no complaints from anyone.

But suddenly it all changed. Just before midday on one of those interminable October firsts, Crompton saw a smudge of oily black smoke on the horizon, and heard a rumble of ominous thunder to the west. Coming down from his ranchstyle presidential palace to investigate, Crompton saw column after column of panzer tanks moving down South Orange Avenue. Standing in the foremost tank was Field Marshal Erwin Rommel. Standing beside Rommel and looking very pleased with himself was Daniel Stack.

Then Crompton remembered. This was supposed to be a fight to the death via simulation. While he had been fooling around, Stack had been busy creating Rommel and the Afrika Korps.

It looked as though this war might be over before it had properly begun.

There was no time to make a plan. Crompton snatched at the first images that came to him, conjuring up a fifty-man Swiss guard armed with pikes, a boatload of Viking berserkers, and a detachment of Hungarian irregular cavalry led by von Suppe. These light forces held the approaches to South Mountains Reservation at the Wyoming Avenue line for twenty minutes, long enough for Crompton flee to the south.

Stack came thundering after him, his armor cutting through the confused Etruscans, Waziris, Dayaks, Janissaries, and Amboinese that Crompton threw in his path. As he advanced, Stack took control of the metamorphized dream territory of the conflict, changing it into western France and pinning Crompton against the sea at Cherbourg. As Stack reorganized his forces for the killing stroke, Crompton threw all his remaining strength into a last effort.

He managed to wrestle control of the dream territory from Stack, with him on one side of the Guadarrama Mountains and Stack on the other.

Stack was stopped for the moment. Crompton took advantage of the precious respite to simulate fresh troops.

Hastily he created Varus's lost legion led by Gustavus Adolphus, and a double regiment of Assyrian axmen led by Hammurabi. He knew that these forces were hopelessly inadequate—but the swiftness and fury of Stack's assault left him no time to ponder military metaphors. Under pressure, he had to use whatever frivolous images his crossword-loving mind sent up. It put him at a considerable disadvantage, since Stack's natural orientation was toward gory visions and bloody spectacles.

But now the situation changes again. Stack solves the territorial problem by converting his panzers into an enormous army of blank-faced Aztecs armed with sound-swords and wivver pistols, and led by Tezcatlipoca. These forces scramble down the steep Guadarrama slopes on knotted vines, screaming bird-call war cries and making hateful faces.

Crompton's Assyrians take one look and head back to

Babylon as fast as their dromedaries can carry them. Varus's lost legion close shields and hold their ground. Soon they are engulfed in a sea of copper warriors. Desperately Crompton sends in Tom Mix, Billy the Kid, the Magnificent Seven, Joe Louis, and Teddy Roosevelt's Rough Riders. They are swallowed up piecemeal, and Crompton reels back, exhausted, finished. . . .

Only to be rescued by the provident arrival of Loomis, who comes charging out of a glade of oak trees with five thousand Kashmiri hashisheens.

Stack contains this thrust by creating and interposing the Membrillo Apaches, with two Zulu impis in support. Loomis is repulsed with heavy losses. But Stack has overreached himself, he falters, his forces waver and slide in and out of focus. Crompton takes over the territoriality motif and creates a wide summer meadow, just the place for the ten squadrons of Cromwell's Roundheads that he has simulated.

Stack reacts quickly by changing the meadow into a desert and charging in with Genghis Khan and his horde. Crompton mows them down with machine-gun fire from the destroyer he has just produced on the lake he has just created.

Stack simulates Submariner and sinks the cruiser. He decimates Crompton's forces with hard-bitten Carthaginian cohorts. His troops devastate the countryside. They catch Loomis feasting in the greenwood and seem likely to destroy him. But at the last moment, who should join the fight but Finch, mounted on a white elephant at the right hand of King Asoka, marching with a colorful collection of mantra-singing bodhisattvas, arahants, and pratyekabuddhas. These forces refuse to kill anyone and confine themselves to scornful glances: they are easily obliterated by Stack's fuzzy-wuzzies. But their interposition gives Loomis time to change into Owen Glendower and vanish into the mountains of Wales.

In the resulting confusion, Crompton takes charge. He transposes the situation into the American Civil War, producing the lines outside Richmond and splitting himself into Grant and Sherman. Stack's feeble riposte is to turn into Chief Joseph of the Nez Percé and retreat toward Canada. He makes a stand at Mindanao, which falls, and then at Dien Bien Phu, which also falls.

Pressed to the utmost extremity, Stack is heard to mutter: "I'm a Freud that this day that began so Jung is getting Adler and Adler. . . ."

He goes down at last into a flaming pit of oblivion that Crompton has created for him. His qualities are reduced to notions, his essence is denied.

Loomis is looking for a truce now, his spaniel-brown eyes begging; but Crompton, full of end-state lust, impales him on a crimson derationalizer.

Finch doesn't even wait to be struck down. To save Crompton from murder, he reverts to nothingness.

They are gone now, all gone. And now it is Crompton alone, thick breath sobbing in his throat, staring at the carnage and watching himself change change change into implacable archetypal killer weeping in his beer and throwing up all over his glen-plaid suit. A definitive Crompton for the ages!

But now, lo, Crompton himself is gone. He is here no longer with his schemes and desires, his hopes and fears, his talented nose and scrawny body.

There is someone else here. It is a new time, and now a new person has been created through the wonder of the alchemical marriage.

The new person opened his eyes and yawned and stretched, enjoying the sensations of light and color. Former possession of Alistair Crompton, tenanted for a while by Edgar Loomis, Dan Stack, and Barton Finch, the new person stood up and considered life and found it good. Integrated at last, like other men, he could not be multifarious, many-motived. At last he could strive for the important things in life—sex, money, love, and God—and still have time left for several hobbies.

What should he strive for first? How about money and God, and let love work itself out? How about going all out for love and money, and letting the God thing sit for a while?

He considered. No solution came to mind. He saw that there were many things to do, and many things to not do, and there were many reasons for doing and not doing each thing, and there was no clear way of knowing what was right and what was not.

The new person considered. A presentiment of disaster came over him. He was still stuck in the human situation! He said, "Hey, Alistair, fellows, are you still there? I don't think this one is going to work either."

ABOUT THE AUTHOR

Long considered one of the wittiest of established science fiction writers—with a remarkable facility for plot twists, offbeat humor, and idiosyncratic style—ROBERT SHECKLEY has published a large body of short fiction and seven other novels, most recently, *Mindswap, Dimension of Miracles, Options* and *Crompton Divided.* Born in New York, his work in the field of science fiction dates from 1951. Mr. Sheckley currently resides in London.

OUT OF THIS WORLD!

That's the only way to describe Bantam's great series of
science fiction classics. These space-age thrillers are filled
with terror, fancy and adventure and written by America's
most renowned writers of science fiction. Welcome to outer
space and have a good trip!

FANTASY AND SCIENCE FICTION FAVORITES

Bantam brings you the recognized classics as well as the current favorites in fantasy and science fantasy. Here you will find the beloved Conan books along with recent titles by the most respected authors in the genre.